UnCOVEReD!

Weird
weird
stories

Puffin Books

UnCOVEReD!

What the experts say:

'When my teacher reads your stories to my class, sometimes she's laughing so hard she can't finish the sentence. And for my teacher to laugh you're real magical.' **Cristina**, *New York*

'The writing is so excellent and so real it is just like watching a movie.' **Nisrene**, *Condell Park, New South Wales*

'You are a weird, wacky, wonderful, ~~funny~~, no, make that hilarious writer.' **Shannon**, *New Plymouth, New Zealand*

'You are a cool and mad writer.' **Zoe**, *Leeming, Western Australia*

'You have brought much pleasure and joy to my life and a desire to read my way through libraries.' **Patricia** (aged 43!), *Beaumaris, Victoria*

'When I read your books I laugh until my head rolls off.' **Claire**, *Warwickshire, U.K.*

PAUL JENNINGS

UnCoVeReD!

Weird
Weird
stories

Puffin Books

Puffin Books
Penguin Books Australia Ltd
487 Maroondah Highway, PO Box 257
Ringwood, Victoria 3134, Australia
Penguin Books Ltd
Harmondsworth, Middlesex, England
Viking Penguin, A Division of Penguin Books USA Inc.
375 Hudson Street, New York, New York 10014, USA
Penguin Books Canada Limited
10 Alcorn Avenue, Toronto, Canada M4V 3B2
Penguin Books (NZ) Ltd
182–190 Wairau Road, Auckland 10, New Zealand

First published by Penguin Books Australia, 1995
10 9 8 7 6 5 4 3

Typeset in 10/13 Baskerville by Midland Typesetters, Maryborough, Victoria
Printed in England by Clays Ltd, St Ives plc

National Library of Australia
Cataloguing-in-Publication data:

Jennings, Paul, 1943–
Uncovered!: Weird weird stories.

ISBN 0 14 036900 7

1. Children's stories, Australia. I. Title.

A823.3

To George Dale,
with thanks for the
many great book designs

CONTENTS

FOR EVER

1

Every kid in the class was laughing at Richard.

Well, everyone except Tim. He felt more like crying. After all, Richard was his brother.

Even Ms Fish, the teacher, had to bite her tongue to stop herself chuckling. She stared out of the window, watching Richard leap around in the playground. 'Tim,' she said.

Tim sighed. Then he picked up his crutches and swung his way to the door. Another gale of laughter rocked the room as he left. Richard was at it again. Toilet paper. Why was Richard so mad about toilet paper? Why couldn't it be newspaper? Or paper bags? Why did it always have to be toilet paper?

Today it was worse than usual.

In the past Richard had wrapped up letter-boxes and sticks and garden spades. But today took the cake. Richard had wrapped himself. He looked like a mummy risen from the dead. Bound head to foot in toilet paper. Loose bits flapped in the breeze as he danced around the playground.

Tim hobbled across the yard. 'Come on,' he said gently to his brother. 'Come back inside.'

'Aargh, aargh, aargh,' barked Richard.

'Aargh' was his only word. If you could call it a word. Richard had never spoken a sensible sentence in his life.

As Tim approached, Richard pranced around like a dog when someone tries to take a ball from its mouth. He darted in and out – wanting and not wanting to be caught at the same time.

'Oh no,' Tim said as he saw Richard glance at a nearby gum tree.

Tim tried to shepherd his brother away. But the crutches and his tired arms slowed him down. In a flash Richard was scrambling up the tree trunk.

Tim suddenly felt very tired. The crutches chafed his armpits. And his head throbbed. The pain that always gnawed at his chest was worse than ever. He lowered himself to the grass. 'Please come down, Richard,' he said. 'I can't climb trees.'

'Aargh, aargh, aargh,' barked Richard.

Tim looked towards the school. The teachers had agreed to give Richard a trial. Two months to see if they could handle him. If not, he would have to find another school. Tim shook his head. Nobody could handle Richard. Except Tim. He had to think of something. Otherwise there would be a fuss. And Richard wouldn't be allowed to stay. 'Come on, Richard,' he yelled. 'Please come down.'

2

The bell rang and kids started streaming out into the yard. Soon there was a big circle standing around the tree. Laughing, pointing, joking. Richard waved a white toilet roll in one bandaged hand.

'Please don't,' Tim said to himself.

Richard started to unroll his treasure. Soon a long ribbon was fluttering out from his arm. Longer and longer like a never-ending flag. Flapping and waving in the sunshine. Finally it broke. The wind caught the fragile paper and lifted it above the head of the crowd. Kids jumped and reached, yelling and laughing. The toilet paper twisted and snaked towards the school. Finally it drifted down and the mob grabbed it wildly, pulling the sheets apart and throwing them into the wind.

Richard swung around in the tree like a ghostly monkey. He began pulling his paper bandage away and throwing it down on the laughing mob of kids.

Tim's heart dropped as he saw teachers coming with a ladder. He had to get Richard down before they frightened him. Otherwise he might fall on someone. Or hurt himself. If that happened Richard might be sent home. For good.

Tim closed his eyes and tried to shut out the angry blood-red clouds that swirled inside his head.

'Think of snow,' he said to himself.

A wonderful picture filled his mind. Soft, silent flakes of snow fell gently to the ground. Imaginary houses carried banks of whiteness. Every branch bowed beneath a cold burden. A snowman stood watching without a word. Peace. Nothing disturbed this wintry peace.

Now Tim knew what to do. The snow had never let him down.

2

Tim opened his eyes. Teachers were hustling across the yard with a ladder. Kids were jumping and shouting, enjoying the show. He had to hurry. He limped towards the tree on his crutches and then started fishing around in his pocket. 'Hurry, hurry, hurry,' he said to himself. And then, 'Got 'em.'

He pulled out two squashed sachets of honey that his Dad had brought back from a motel. The type that have just enough for one slice of toast. Tim quickly pushed them both into a hole in the side of the tree. 'Hey, what's this in here?' he called in a loud voice. He pretended to be very interested in the hole. Out of the side of one eye he could see Richard peering down. 'Oh, look,' he shouted to himself. 'Honey.' He pulled out one sachet and made a great show of peeling back the lid and slurping the contents. He sucked and chewed noisily.

Richard watched from above.

'I wonder if there's any more,' Tim yelled into the hole.

In a flash Richard dropped lightly to the ground and thrust his hand into the tree. He pulled out the sachet and shoved it into his mouth without opening it. He munched happily, not knowing or caring that the whole school was watching. Finally he spat out the plastic container.

'Well done, Tim,' said Ms Fish.

The two boys headed for the classroom. Tim paused as a pain growled inside his chest. He winced and then kept going. He wondered how long the teachers would go on letting Richard disturb the class. He didn't seem to be learning anything at all. And he was annoying everyone else.

That night Richard sat in the corner of the lounge and fiddled with a toilet roll. He turned it over and over and over. He seemed hardly aware that Tim and his mother and father were in the room.

Dad tossed Richard two sachets of honey. 'Here,' he said. 'Give one to Tim.'

Richard turned them over in his hand. He looked at Tim for just a second and then shoved both into his mouth.

'Aren't you going to share?' said Mum.

'A bit late for that,' Tim grinned. He gave Richard a friendly punch. 'One day,' Tim told him. 'One day me and you are going to the snow.' He closed his eyes and described what he saw. Richard fiddled with the toilet paper, not taking his gaze from it for a second.

'That snow,' said Tim, 'is as fresh as an apple still on the tree. It is as cool as the breeze across a deep, deep lake. Oh, I see that snow like it is here now. Me and you are there, Richard. We are sliding down the slope on skis. And there is a snowman. And you know what? You know what that snowman is doing, Richard? You know what that snowman is doing? Is he just standing there? Is he just silent under the blue sky?

'No. That snowman is dancing, Richard.

'Oh, you should see him. He is leaping around and

5

skipping and throwing up his arms. He is picking up snow and throwing it into the air. Oh, that snowman. He is full of joy. He doesn't care that the sun will melt him away. He doesn't worry about what is coming. He is king of the snow. There is no tomorrow for him. Oh, look at him dance, look at him dance.'

Tim smiled beneath his closed eyes.

'We will see him, Richard. We will. You and me. One day we will see snow. One day we will go to the mountains. One day we will see the snowman dance.'

Tim opened his eyes and the snow-covered scene vanished. 'I'm going to lie down,' he said. 'I don't feel too good.' He picked up his crutches and swung out of the room.

Richard turned over the toilet roll. Over and over. 'Aargh, aargh, aargh,' he said.

The boys' mum and dad looked at each other with tear-filled eyes.

'Tim will never see snow,' said Mum. 'Not in Australia in December.'

'He might make it,' said the father. 'It sometimes snows in the mountains in June.'

'June will be too late,' said Mum.

'I should have taken him last year,' said Dad.

'Don't blame yourself,' said Mum. 'The doctor wouldn't allow it, remember.'

'Aargh, aargh, aargh,' barked Richard. The noise was louder and more violent than usual. He hugged the toilet roll to his chest and rocked like a baby.

Mum glanced over at Richard. 'Do you think he knows?' she said.

Dad scowled as a truck changed gear on the road outside. It sounded its horn loudly. 'He doesn't know about anything. Except toilet rolls. Here we go again.'

Richard's face lit up. He raced out the door. 'Aargh, aargh, aargh.' At the front gate he jumped up and down waving his arms crazily. The truck had a large toilet roll painted on the side. Underneath was written 'SOFT AS DAWN'. The driver leaned over and wound down the passenger side window. Then he threw something into the air.

It turned over and over and then bounced crazily into the front yard.

Richard scampered after his prize. One tightly wrapped roll of toilet paper. He grabbed it eagerly and clutched it to his chest. 'Aargh, aargh, aargh,' he yelled happily.

Another truck rounded the corner and the driver also threw out a toilet roll. He tooted and laughed as Richard gathered up the bouncing paper. A third and a fourth truck did the same. Each driver enjoyed this daily ritual. Passers-by stopped and stared at the strange sight.

Richard ran back inside with the loot. He headed towards his favourite place. The loft. A large, warm space in the roof of the house. He climbed up the ladder and disappeared through a manhole.

3

'Geeze, I don't know,' said Dad. 'All these blasted toilet rolls. We have to put a stop to it. It's just making him worse. We're the laughing stock of the neighbourhood.

Harry James asked me if we're going to build a public toilet in the front yard. I'll bet the factory doesn't know their drivers are throwing away rolls and rolls every day. It's been going on for years.'

'Have you looked at his face?' said Mum. 'It's the only time Richard ever smiles. When those toilet rolls come bouncing over the fence he's happy. You can't stop that.'

'It's a fire risk,' said Dad. 'All that paper up inside the roof. The whole place could go up in smoke.'

'Think of it as free insulation,' said Mum.

'Have you been up there lately? Go and have a look. And don't let him see you or you'll cop the usual.'

Mum silently climbed the ladder and peered in the loft. Her eyes widened. A huge castle made of toilet rolls filled the entire space. It was so much bigger than before. Turrets and walls and a tall, arched entrance. Paper stairs made their way to the top of the ramparts. Dolls and teddy bears were propped up like archers peering down at the enemy. The whole loft was crammed with thousands and thousands of toilet rolls.

'Aargh, aargh, aargh.' Richard's face appeared over the battlements. He began to fire on the intruder. A shower of bouncing toilet rolls peppered Mum. She quickly ducked down and closed the loft hatch above her.

'Right,' yelled Dad. 'That's it. I'm not putting up with this nonsense for one more second.' He climbed quickly up the ladder and opened the hatch. 'Richard, get down from there. I'm putting a stop to this. Tomorrow I'm going to the factory to stop those drivers throwing out toilet rolls. And all of this is going. Every last one. It's ridiculous. Now come down here at once.'

'Aargh, aargh, aargh.' Toilet rolls fell around Dad like mortar shells. He shook his fist at Richard as the angry boy lobbed the rolls over the castle walls. Dad ducked and hit his head on the side of the hatch. Then he fell, screaming and grabbing at the rungs of the ladder. He crashed heavily to the floor.

'Damn and blast,' he yelled.

Mum tried to smother a smile. 'Are you okay, dear?' she asked.

'No I'm not. It's not funny. I mean it. Every last bit of paper is going out of that loft.'

Another hailstorm of toilet rolls bounced down on top of him and the hatch banged shut.

4

In his room nearby, Tim lay on his bed and listened to the commotion. He shook his head. He knew what the toilet roll castle meant to Richard. Terrible things would happen if he lost the toilet rolls. He had been collecting them for years. Building with them. Wrapping things up. His loft was a refuge. A place to go. A warm world of his own. Angry red clouds rolled in Tim's head. Why couldn't Richard talk? Why did he always have to live in a lonely world of his own?

Tim looked at his crutches propped against the bed. Life wasn't fair. He closed his eyes. And thought of snow.

Gentle, falling snow. Drifting down. Cleaning the world with its whiteness. Covering the streets and the cars. Happy children threw snowballs and laughed.

And there he was. The best bit of all. The snowman. Dancing, dancing. Lifting his black hat with a snowy arm. Winking with his coal-black eyes. Beckoning Tim. Calling him. 'Oh, look at that snowman dance,' said Tim. A wonderful peace filled his mind. He lay back on his pillow and for a while the pain in his chest melted away.

'I'd love to see snow,' he said to himself. 'If I could see snow. Just once. I'd be happy for ever.'

Tim opened his eyes and the vision vanished. Outside the window the summer sun cooked the brown grass.

'Oh no,' said Tim.

A figure was loping across the lawn, dragging a large garbage bag behind him. 'Aargh, aargh, aargh,' said Richard.

Tim could see that Richard was angry. He knew that his brother was running away from home. Taking his most precious possessions with him.

'Come back, Richard,' yelled Tim. But he was too late. Richard had already disappeared along the footpath. Tim struggled out of bed and searched frantically for his shoes. Where were they? Under the bed. He grabbed a crutch and hooked them out. He quickly put on the shoes and limped outside. 'Richard, Richard,' he yelled. His voice echoed along the empty street. Richard was nowhere to be seen.

Tim set off along the road. His crutches rubbed under his arm and with every step the pain in his chest grew worse. He knew that he was supposed to take it easy. Not strain himself. 'Richard,' he called. 'Richard.'

Tim was worried. He should have told Mum and Dad

so they could use the car to search. But Dad was angry with Richard. This might be the last straw.

Richard could be in danger. He would often run across roads without looking. At this very moment he might be on top of someone's roof. Or hanging off a bridge over a river. Or crawling down a drain.

Blood-red clouds began to swirl in Tim's mind. But there was no time to call the snowman to drive them away. Sweat began to form on his brow and he felt faint.

5

Tim wandered the streets for hours. Up and down. Along and around. He couldn't find Richard anywhere. He had tried all of the usual places. The bridge. The station. The river. Nothing.

Finally Tim leaned his crutches on a wall and sat down. He felt very, very tired. He had just decided to give up and go home when something caught his eye. A letter-box. A letter-box wrapped in toilet paper.

Richard had been this way.

Tim struggled on. A dog ran past. A dog wrapped up in a paper bandage. This dog had met Richard for sure.

The houses gave way to fields. A herd of black cows grazed lazily in the sunshine. Twenty black cows. And one white one. A farmer was cursing and pulling away the shroud of paper which entwined his mooing animal.

Tim hobbled on, following the paper trail. He found it hard to breathe. He was hot and the pain in his chest grew worse and worse. But he kept going. He had to.

Finally he stopped. A long stream of paper fluttered in the gutter. It wound like a country road through the long, brown grass to a barbed-wire fence. A few strands of paper were impaled on the wire. The trail led through the fence and onto . . .

'The train line,' gasped Tim. He rolled under the fence and climbed up onto the tracks. Cold sweat formed on his brow as he followed the steel and paper trail. His breath came in gasps. His chest seemed to be enclosed in a ring of iron which grew tighter and tighter. The tips of his crutches slipped and jarred on the heavy stones between the tracks.

Tim knew what lay around the corner. He tried not to think about it. 'Think of snow,' he said to himself. 'Think of snow.' But the snow would not come. The dancing snowman had deserted him. There was nothing but angry, red clouds. And a railway line running across a tall, tall bridge.

In the centre of the bridge a tiny figure danced crazily, waving a long, white stream of paper. A fragile rope which suddenly broke and fell uncaringly into the river far, far below.

6

Tim stopped when he reached the bridge. It stood on huge wooden legs which spanned the river beneath. At the top it was narrow with one set of tracks which ran along close to the edge.

Gentle vibrations, growing strongly, came up through

Tim's crutches. The train was somewhere on the other side of the bridge. Tim wanted to run onto the bridge and grab his brother. But he knew in his heart that if he did, neither of them would come back.

'Richard,' he screamed. 'Richard. The train is coming. This way, quick. Get off the bridge.' He took one wobbling step towards his brother but could go no further. One crutch lodged in a gap in the planks. Tim fell sprawling between the tracks. His chest hurt terribly. And one leg was bleeding freely. For a second he just wanted to stay there. Just stop and let things happen. Blood-red clouds swirled. He lay back and shook his head. Then he closed his eyes.

'Where are you?' he said. 'Where are you? Don't let me down now.'

And through the mists of his mind came the wonderful, dancing snowman. Calling, calling, calling. Beckoning with a snowy finger.

Tim smiled. He opened his eyes and crawled towards his crutches which were balanced on one of the rails. He moved his fingers like the legs of a spider. He could just reach the crutches and scratch them towards himself. In a second he had them and was up on his feet. The vibrations from the tracks grew stronger and stronger. He looked towards the other side. In the distance a train whistle sounded.

'Richard,' he shouted. 'This is for you.' He rummaged in his pocket and pulled out a sachet of honey. He lifted his arm and threw with all his might. The tiny container arced into the air and then fell down, down, down until it disappeared in the pebbles by the river.

The train was on the bridge. Thundering towards

Richard. Brakes screaming. Sparks flying high into the air.

Richard looked down after the honey. He looked at Tim. He looked at the train behind him. 'Aargh, aargh, aargh,' he screamed. Then he ran, stumbling towards his brother. Fleeing before the steel monster which screeched and roared towards him. He fell at Tim's feet.

The train was upon them. Richard peered down the grassy slope towards the river, searching with his eyes for the honey. Then he jumped off the tracks and bounded over the fence and down the hill.

Tim had no strength. He simply fell, like a tree teetering after the axeman's last blow. He toppled sideways, away from the train. The thundering wheels crunched his crutches to splinters. Tim rolled like a log. Down the gentle bank and under the fence. At last he stopped by a small stand of bushes.

'Aargh, aargh, aargh,' came Richard's voice from the river far below. He scrabbled among the rocks, looking for the honey.

'Stupid little idiots,' came a fading voice from the last carriage of the train as it rushed into the distance.

Richard struggled back up to his brother with the sachet of honey. He held it out in one hand. But Tim was too tired to even notice.

7

Later, at home, the doctor pulled the sheet back up to Tim's chin and looked at the sleeping figure. 'He's a very sick little boy,' he said to the two parents. 'He must have walked ten kilometres. On crutches. And that fall down the bank. It was too much for him. It was getting near the time anyway. You should think about putting him into hospital soon.'

Tim's dad shook his head. 'We've talked about this over and over,' he said. 'We knew this day was going to come. And we're ready for it. We want him to spend his last days in his own bed. At home with us.'

Above their heads, in the bedroom ceiling, an eye swivelled and stared down through a small hole. The eye moistened and formed a tiny droplet. The tear wobbled for a second and then fell. It spun glistening through the warm air and plopped onto Tim's cheek. His mother wiped it away, thinking it was her son's. She was right. And she was wrong. 'He's crying in his sleep,' she said. The eye in the ceiling blinked.

'He wanted to see the snow,' said Dad. 'He's never been to the snow. He's never seen a snowman. Or a snowstorm. It's the only thing he's ever wanted.'

They all looked out of the window. Insects buzzed in the warm summer air.

'And now he never will,' said Mum. 'I wish he could see snow before he ...' She found it almost impossible to say the word. 'Dies.'

The eye in the ceiling vanished. A terrible banging and crashing came from above. A long barking howl filled the air. 'Aaaargh, aaaaargh, aaaargh.'

'What on earth ...?' said the doctor.

They all looked up at the ceiling. 'It's Richard,' said Dad. 'He's had a bad day. Don't worry. I'll get him down. He'll be okay.'

After the doctor had gone Dad climbed the ladder to the loft. The noise grew worse and worse. Dad pushed up the hatch and peered inside. A hail of toilet rolls drove him back.

'What's happening?' said Mum.

'He's gone crazy. He's completely wrecked his castle. Demolished the whole thing. Toilet rolls are everywhere.'

Suddenly the noise stopped. Mum climbed the ladder and peeped in.

'Well?' said Dad.

'He's angry about something,' said Mum. 'He's sitting there with a toilet roll. He's pulling it to shreds. Just biting it and ripping it to bits like a wild animal.'

She quietly lowered the hatch and climbed down.

'Do you think he knows?' said Dad. 'About Tim?'

'Who knows what he knows,' said Mum. 'But just for once we are going to have to forget about Richard. And worry about Tim.'

8

Two days passed and Tim grew weaker and weaker.

In the ceiling above all was quiet. Richard refused to come down. Every time the hatch was lifted a furious hail of toilet rolls met the intruder.

'Just leave him,' said Dad. 'He'll get sick of it up there and he'll come down like he always does.'

'He's hardly touched the food I put up there,' said Mum. 'But I've got something special. I've been keeping it for an emergency.' She fetched a two-litre jar of honey from the kitchen. 'This ought to bring him down.' She climbed the ladder and carefully lifted the hatch. Then she waved the honey jar through the opening. 'Richard,' she said softly. 'Look what I've got.'

There was no reply. Then, before she could blink the honey disappeared. Snatched from her hand. 'Rats,' she yelled. 'He's grabbed it. Now he'll never come down. We'll just have to leave him.'

Both parents went down to Tim's room. They were shocked by what they saw. 'Get the doctor,' said Dad. Tim was pale and sweaty. His eyes rolled wildly in his head and his breath came in heavy gasps.

Above them in the ceiling an eye stared down and then disappeared.

Outside the warm summer breeze was swinging around and becoming cooler.

The doctor arrived within twenty minutes and gave Tim an injection. 'Stay with him,' he said. 'I'll wait in the lounge. It's not going to be long now.'

Tim opened his eyes and tried to sit up. His father lifted him so that he sat upright on the pillows. 'I want to look out,' said Tim. 'At the garden.'

His father pushed the bed until it was hard up against the window. Without warning something crashed onto the path outside.

Dad stared out. 'A tile,' he gasped. 'A tile's come off the roof.' Another tile hurtled down and smashed into a thousand pieces. And then another and another.

'It's Richard,' said Mum. 'He's on the roof. And he's wrecking the place.'

Like a furious fiend Richard grabbed tile after tile and

threw them to the ground. Then he crawled up and over to the other side of the roof. He grabbed tiles wildly and tossed them into the air. Soon there was a yawning hole on both sides of the roof.

The wind dropped completely. It was the stillness that always comes before a cool change in Melbourne.

9

And still the tiles fell.

'Get the fire brigade,' said Mum. 'We have to get him down.'

'No,' said Dad. 'This is one time when Richard is not getting all the attention.' He took his wife's hand and led her back to their fevered son.

'What's going on?' said Tim weakly.

'Nothing for you to worry about,' said Dad. 'You just lie back there and think about . . . '

'Snow,' said Mum softly. She nodded through the door at the doctor. He quietly left the room and went outside.

He placed a ladder against the wall and climbed to the top. 'Good grief,' he said as he stared into the roofless house. He turned and scrambled back down. He beckoned to Mum through the window.

'What's up?' she whispered.

'He's taken off all his clothes,' said the doctor. 'And he's smeared honey all over himself. And those toilet rolls. He's . . . '

A cold breeze stirred and turned into a gust.

'He's torn up all those toilet rolls into little scraps. There's not one left.'

The gust became a gale. And lifted a billion tiny pieces of toilet paper into the air.

From his bed by the window Tim's eyes grew wide. He stared in amazement at the eddying cloud of white flakes.

'Snow,' Tim choked. 'Oh, it's snowing. Oh, just look at that snow. That snow,' said Tim, 'is as fresh as an apple still on the tree. It's as cool as the breeze across a deep, deep lake. Oh, I thought I'd never see it.'

Another gust lifted the paper and drove it crazy like a billion white bees swarming in furious silence over a winter garden.

Then the wind dropped. And the paper began to settle. It filled the air and flurried down covering the brown grass with a snow-white coat. Branches bowed in reverence. The car disappeared like a cake under Christmas icing.

Drifts formed on the window. Distant houses vanished under the swirling clouds. The world was white, white, white.

'Look,' called Tim. 'Look. Yes, it is. I'm sure it is. A snowman. Oh, can you see that snowman?'

And there, faintly emerging from his private storm, was Richard. Paper stuck to the honey. A wild, snowy figure. Prancing and dancing amongst the flurries. The finest snowman ever. Dressed in a warm, white coat.

Tim gazed in wonder as his dream came true before his staring eyes. 'Just look at that,' he said in wonder. 'A snowman. Look at him go.' He gave a happy laugh.

His last laugh.

He lay back on the pillows with an enormous smile on his face.

His last smile.

Then he closed his eyes for the last time.

And went off to dance with the snowman.

For ever.

TOO MANY RABBITS

1

Sex is not talked about in our place. No one has told me anything. I have worked out quite a few things myself though. I keep my ears open and my eyes to the ground.

I know the main bits. I see things. Like when Sky's dog had pups. One day Sandy was fat and there were no puppies and the next day she was thin and there they were. You don't have to be too smart to work out where they came from.

How they got in there, I even know that too.

Sandy is a great dog. And the puppies are beautiful. I would like one of them more than anything in the world. But I just can't talk Dad around. He will not have any pets at all.

'Can I have a pet, Dad?' I asked him.

'What sort of pet?' he said.

'A dog?'

'Nah, they bark too much. And they dig holes and annoy the neighbours.'

'A cat?' I said.

'Nah, they leave fur everywhere.'

'A bird?'

'Nah, it's cruel to keep them in cages.'

'A mouse?' I begged.

'Nah, they breed like rabbits.'

'An elephant,' I yelled.

Dad grinned at this. 'If you can find one you can have it,' he said.

I raced out and grabbed Saturday's paper. Before he changed his mind. You have to strike while the lion is hot. I looked and looked but there were no elephants for sale. Not one. I bet that Dad knew this all along. Parents can be so sneaky sometimes.

After this I was sent to my room for throwing the paper on the floor and yelling.

We live in a bookshop in the main street. Upstairs is Mum and Dad's room. Under that is the shop. Down the bottom is the storeroom and my bedroom. There are no windows in my room. It's like a jail. I am always getting sent to my room. It's not fair.

If I was to dig a hole in the wall I could make a tunnel. I could escape. Like prisoners of war do.

It would be great to have an escape tunnel. Even if it took me twenty years to dig, I would have a way out when I was sent to my room. It would be worth it in the long run.

Anyway, there I was lying on my bed and not allowed out. I just stared at the wall. It was made out of wooden panels. There was nothing else to do so I decided to pull a panel off and start to dig into the wall behind it. I started pushing at the wood with an old screwdriver. I put the blade in a crack and levered.

Bingo. Kerpow. Wow. The panel just swung open. Just like that. It was a door. A secret door. I couldn't believe it. I didn't have to dig a tunnel. There was already something there.

I stared into the hole but I couldn't see a thing. It was dark. And musty. It smelled all stale. I wanted to go straight in and explore. But I didn't have a torch. It might be dangerous.

No, this would take a bit of thinking about. I wouldn't go in until I could get a torch. There could be horrible things lying around. I could hurt myself in the dark. It's important to look before you weep.

I shut the door and waited for my time in solitary confinement to be over.

2

The following day I went next door to see Sky. She owned a junk shop and I knew she would have an old torch somewhere. You could find wonderful things in that shop.

Sky grinned when I asked her. 'A torch? I don't know, love. There might be one in the corner over there.'

I rummaged around for ages. Beads, candles, bits of broken bikes, one thong, hats, a cracked toilet seat, a knife with no handle, a rabbit in a cage.

A rabbit in a cage.

A beautiful, lovely, pink-eyed rabbit with a black patch on its white back. 'Wow,' I said. 'This is the most beautiful rabbit in the world. I wish it was mine.' I pressed its warm fur up to my face.

'Ten dollars,' said Sky. 'You can have it for ten dollars. That's what I paid for it.'

I shook my head. 'Dad will never let me have it,' I said. 'Anyway, I haven't got ten dollars.'

Sky smiled at me kindly. 'You can have it for eight,' she said. 'I can't say fairer than that. But you'll have to be quick. I had six yesterday and this is the last one left.'

I spent ages stroking the rabbit. 'Pinky,' I said. 'Her name is Pinky and she loves me.'

'I've only got ten cents on me,' I said. 'But I've got eight dollars at home.' I knew that Dad wouldn't let me keep the rabbit but I had an idea. I would hide Pinky. Dad would never know.

But where? Where could I hide her?

Of course. The space behind the wall. You could keep a rabbit in there and no one would know. But first I would need a torch.

'What about this?' said Sky. She had a torch in her hand. Not a bad one either. And it had batteries that worked.

'How much?' I asked.

Sky was wearing about a hundred strings of bright beads around her neck. She always fiddled with them when she was with a customer. 'Ten cents,' she said.

'Gee thanks,' I said. I put Pinky down and ran back into our bookshop. I was in such a hurry that I bumped straight into Dad. Oh no, he was going to ask me what I wanted a torch for.

'Where'd you get that?' said Dad. 'It's a nice-looking torch.'

'I bought it from Sky,' I said. 'Ten cents.'

'Ten cents,' said Dad. 'It's worth at least ten dollars. No wonder she's going broke.'

'What?' I said.

'She's got no money. She's behind with the rent. She feels sorry for people and sells everything for less than she bought it for. They'll kick her out soon for sure.'

'Who will?' I said.

'The bank. The bank owns all these shops along here.'

The bank was right next door. 'They can't kick her out,' I yelled. 'She's my friend.'

'We're not doing so well ourselves,' said Dad.

I ran down to my room and slammed the door. I was very upset about Sky. I looked at the torch. The torch. The tunnel. I had forgotten all about them.

I switched on the torch and stepped through the wall.

3

It was a big, dark cellar. The floor and three of the walls were concrete. The wall at the back was just dirt and stones. There was nothing there except cobwebs, dust and an old bookshelf with two ancient bird books in it.

Books. My heart sank. I had been hoping for treasure or jewels. I snooped around for a bit but there was nothing to be found. There was a light switch and I turned it on. No, there was nothing to see. Just a cold, gloomy cellar. Still, it would be great for a rabbit. I wouldn't even have to build a cage.

I looked up. Over the top was our shop. On one side was Sky's junk shop. And on the other was the bank. I just stood there thinking. That's when I got the idea. That's when it popped into my head. I could dig a tunnel.

And rob the bank.

Like Robbing Hood. You take from the rich and give to the poor. The bank was rich. Sky was poor. I would take some money and give it to Sky. I wouldn't keep any for myself. Not even eight dollars for a rabbit. I would give it all to Sky. Then she could give it back to the bank and they wouldn't kick her out of her shop. They would get their money back and everybody would be happy.

I smuggled Pinky in and she sniffed around her new home. I could tell that she liked it.

It was a good plan and I made a start straight away. I borrowed Dad's spade and started to dig at the wall. The spade was heavy and the wall was hard. All rocks and stones. After about an hour I stopped. My hands were blistered and sore. I was sweaty and tired. And I had hardly made a scratch on the wall.

Digging tunnels is hard work.

I picked up Pinky and gave her a cuddle. She was very, very fat. She nibbled at my hand. 'She wants food,' I said to myself. I went upstairs and raided the fridge. Two carrots. Pinky finished them off in no time at all. Talk about hungry. And fat. 'Your thighs are bigger than your stomach,' I said.

The next day I took the eight dollars in to Sky. 'Thanks,' she said. 'It's my only sale for the day.' She was down in the dumps. Just sitting there munching on an apple.

'Don't worry,' I said. 'They won't kick you out. I've got a plan.'

'What's that, love?' said Sky.

'I'm digging a tunnel into the bank. I'm going to get you some money.'

Sky shook her head. 'No, no, no,' she said. 'You can't do that.'

'Why not? They've got plenty of money.'

'Yes, but it's not ours. It belongs to other people. It wouldn't be right. And anyway, tunnels are dangerous. It might fall in and kill you. If you dig a tunnel I'll have to tell your dad.'

I couldn't believe it. Sky didn't want me to dig a tunnel. I made up my mind not to tell her anything about the secret cellar. Just in case.

'It was a sweet idea, love,' she said. 'But don't worry. Something will turn up. You shouldn't worry yourself too much about money.' She took a big bite out of her apple.

'Yeah,' I said. 'Money is the fruit of all evil.'

I went home and got some straw and rags for Pinky. The floor of the cellar was cold. I also took her another three carrots. She gobbled them down like crazy. Rabbits sure do eat a lot. Especially big fat ones like Pinky.

That night Mum had a few words to say at tea-time. 'Nearly all the carrots have gone,' she said. 'Have you taken them, Philip?'

I nodded my head.

'I'm glad to see you eating vegetables,' she said. 'But please ask first. Yours isn't the only mouth around here.'

She was right about that. When I got down to the cellar there were another eight mouths. Pinky had given birth to eight of the cutest little bunnies you have ever seen. They were pink and hairless and blind and they sucked away at Pinky's teats like crazy. No wonder she was hungry.

I rushed upstairs and took a bunch of celery out of the fridge. Pinky finished it off in ten minutes flat.

There was one thing I knew for sure. Feeding my family was going to be a problem.

5

I named the new bunnies One, Two, Three, Four, Five, Six, Seven and Eight. I couldn't give them real names because I didn't know what sex they were. I found out after a bit that all of them except poor little Eight were females.

Days passed. Weeks passed. Months passed. My little bunnies became big bunnies.

I had four big problems:

1. Sky was going broke and the bank people were talking about tossing her out of her shop.
2. The rabbits were eating more and more and food was hard to find.
3. What goes in one end comes out the other.
4. One, Two, Three, Four, Five, Six and Seven were all getting very fat indeed.

'Times are hard,' said Sky. 'People aren't throwing out their old things. I just haven't got enough stock to sell. The rent costs more than I make.'

I nodded wisely. I was short of money myself. I was spending it all on vegetables for my rabbits. 'It's hard to make lends meet,' I said.

Mum was watching the fridge like a hawk. She counted every carrot. Every leaf of lettuce. She even knew how many peas were in there. 'I think he must have a lack of Vitamin C,' said Mum. 'All he does is eat vegetables and fruit.'

'At least he'll be regular,' said Dad.

Well, things went on like this for quite a bit. Every day I searched for grass, thistles, old cabbage leaves. Anything for my rabbits to eat.

Twice a day I would pull back the secret panel and feed my rabbits. Then I would sweep up the poo and put it out in our tiny backyard.

Dad was starting to get suspicious. 'This is crazy,' said Dad. 'Why are all these rabbits coming into our yard? There are droppings everywhere. Why our place? Why not next door's?'

That night he sat up all night waiting for rabbits. He sat out there in the yard shivering behind some old boxes, waiting and waiting for the rabbits. But none came. 'Something's going on,' he said. 'And I'm going to find out what it is.'

I knew that if he discovered my secret he would give the rabbits away. Or let them go. Or even worse.

Rabbit pie.

That night I found something else. More rabbits. Five

had had six babies. Wonderful, hairless little babies. Still blind with their eyes closed. My little bunnies. It was up to me to look after them. Protect them. Stop Dad finding them.

Two nights later One gave birth. Then Two, Three, Four, Six and Seven followed. My family had grown to thirty-nine wonderful rabbits.

It was great having so many. But going in with the food and out with the poo left no time for anything else. It took over an hour to find grass and thistles and stuff. Mr Griggs from the greengrocer's gave me rotten vegetables but I couldn't take too much. He might tell Dad.

And the poo was becoming a big problem. There was nowhere to put it in the middle of the main street.

One night I watched this movie about prisoners of war digging an escape tunnel. They had to hide the dirt that they dug out. What they did was put the soil in old socks and hide them in their trouser legs. When they pulled on a string the soil would fall out while they were walking along. No one noticed it.

Brainwave. I rubbed my hands together. Truth is stranger than friction.

I filled up two socks with rabbit poo and walked into the street. As I went along the footpath I let a little poo fall to the ground. It worked like a charm. No one noticed.

Well, not at first. 'I can't believe it,' said Dad. 'The whole footpath is covered in rabbit droppings. But you never see a rabbit. Where are they coming from? I'm going to call a meeting of the other shop owners. Something has to be done.'

Two nights later Dad and five of the other shopkeepers sat up watching for the rabbits. Sky told me all about it. 'We waited and waited,' she said. 'In the freezing rain. But not so much as a single rabbit showed up.'

I smiled and shuffled out onto the street to spread a bit more joy around. I was only a kid but I could make things happen. I liked pulling strings.

6

More months went by. My whole life was spent looking after the rabbits. Dirt and sand for the floor. Straw for them to sleep on. Old vegetables and grass for food. Then carting out the poo and dirt and sand and spreading it along the street. It took hours and hours. I had to sneak out at night. In out, in out. The responsibility was getting too much for me.

Then it happened. The next batch of babies. Before I knew it I had one hundred and fifteen rabbits. I couldn't remember their names. I was so tired from carting poo and grass that I could hardly keep my eyes open. The whole thing was turning into a nightmare.

I had to do something.

I sat down and had a good think about my situation. They were all pet rabbits. I couldn't let any go. Foxes and cats would eat them. They didn't know how to look after themselves in the wild. I tried to give a few away at school but the kids' mothers just sent them back. Dad would find out if I kept on with that. But I couldn't let them keep breeding.

How could I stop them?

There was only one way. Keep the males and females apart.

Sky had a second-hand roll of chicken wire. 'You can have it for two dollars,' she said. 'It doesn't matter any more. The bank is closing me down.' Her lips were trembling and her voice was all croaky. I looked at the window. There was a big sign saying: CLOSING DOWN SALE – EVERYTHING CHEAP.

'No,' I yelled. 'You can't leave, Sky. You're my best friend.'

She just shuffled off into the back of the shop so that I wouldn't see her crying.

That afternoon I went into the bank when they were busy and spread some rabbit poo around on the floor. Everyone started sniffing and saying how disgusting it was. As I left I thought I heard someone say something about making a deposit.

After tea I sneaked into the rabbit cellar and built a fence. I put all the males on one side and all the females and babies on the other. It was a good fence. Now there wouldn't be any more babies. 'You are a genius, Philip,' I said to myself.

That night, after feeding the rabbits, I lay down to sleep. All was quiet. For a little while. Then suddenly I heard a terrible squealing noise coming from behind the wall. It grew louder and louder. Squealing and thumping and rustling. It would wake Dad for sure.

'Quiet in there,' I whispered.

The noise grew louder. Oh no. If Dad came down – rabbit pie.

I opened the secret door. A terrible sight met my eyes. The male rabbits were fighting each other. Others were flinging themselves at the fence. Some of the bigger ones were jumping up in the air trying to get over. 'Stop it,' I whispered. 'Stop it.'

But they didn't stop it. More and more male rabbits threw themselves against the fence. They were crazy. They were wild. The fence began to sag. Wham. Down it came. The rabbits poured across like water from a broken dam. Then they started jumping all over each other.

I shut the panel. 'Disgusting,' I said to myself. 'Sex sure is a powerful merge.'

More powerful than I thought. In no time at all I had about four hundred and fifty rabbits.

Things were getting out of hand. The smell was so bad that I could hardly bear to go into the cellar. And it was starting to seep through into my bedroom.

'What's that smell?' said Dad. He sniffed around trying to find something. He looked under the bed and in the cupboard but he didn't find the secret panel. My rabbits were safe. For the time being.

'Make sure you change your socks every day,' Dad said. 'This room smells terrible.'

7

Everything was going wrong. I was facing a mid-wife crisis. I sat down and had a little talk to myself. 'Philip,' I said. 'You can't keep this up. You can't get enough food for the rabbits. You can't keep up with the poo pile. You can't give the rabbits away and you can't keep them. You can't let them go or the foxes will get them. You can't tell Dad and he is going to discover them any day. Sky is getting kicked out of her shop. You are just a kid. You are out of your depth. The rabbits are too much for you. You are too big for your brutes.' My eyes started to water.

There was worse to come. Dad sat next to me on the bed. He saw that I was crying. He took my hand and smiled kindly. 'You've heard then?' he said.

'Heard what?'

'We have to leave the shop. It's not just Sky who can't afford the rent. We've been behind for months. The bank is throwing us out.'

'No,' I screamed. 'No, no, no.' My heart was in my shoes. I didn't want to leave. And I would have to show Dad the rabbits. I couldn't leave them there to starve.

Rabbit pie.

Dad started sniffing around. 'There must be a dead possum in the walls,' he said. 'That smell is disgusting.' He started to tap on the walls, listening and sniffing. He was going to find the rabbits. I just knew he was.

I couldn't bear to watch. I ran up the stairs and into the sunlight. I ran and ran and ran. In the end I was out of breath. I just dropped down onto the footpath and hung my head in my hands.

I couldn't say how long I stayed there. It was a long time. Finally I was driven home by hunger.

When I arrived back I knew straight away that something was wrong. No one was in the shop. Mum and Dad were both downstairs. In my room.

I crept down the stairs. The panel was open. Mum and

Dad were inside the cellar. And the rabbits were gone.

'Murderers,' I yelled.

'What?' said Dad.

'You've killed my rabbits.'

'No,' said Dad. He pulled the old bookshelf away. 'Look at this.'

I couldn't believe it. Amazing. A tunnel. The rabbits had made a break for freedom. They were all gone. Every last one.

'The foxes,' I screamed. 'The foxes will get them.'

I pelted up the stairs.

I looked up the street. I looked down the street. Nothing. Not a rabbit in sight.

Then I looked at Sky's window. The closing-down sign had gone. There was a new one in its place. It said: RABBITS FOR SALE – $15.00 EACH.

The junk shop was full of rabbits. Sky was smiling. There were rabbits everywhere. She even had one on her head. 'I told you something would turn up,' she said. 'They just came out of a hole in the floor. I've sold fifteen already. I'll make a fortune. And I won't have to leave.'

I didn't say anything. There wasn't anything to say. I was happy for Sky. And happy for the rabbits. I smiled and walked slowly back to my room.

'Don't look so gloomy,' said Dad.

'I don't want to leave,' I said. 'I like it here.'

Dad was waving one of the old books I had found.

'We don't have to go,' he yelped. 'You've saved the day, Philip.'

'What?' I mumbled.

'This book. It's a John Gould original. Worth a fortune. We can pay off the bank now, no worries.'

I grinned. I was so happy.

'There's more good news,' said Mum.

'I'm going to have a baby – babies. I'm having twins.'

Geeze, I was happy. Fancy that. Twins. I know why she's having them, too. Mum and Dad own a bookshop. Well, it's obvious, isn't it?

They read like rabbits.

A MOUTHFUL

Parents are embarrassing.

Take my dad. Every time a friend comes to stay the night he does something that makes my face go red. Now don't get me wrong. He is a terrific Dad. I love him but sometimes I think he will never grow up.

He loves playing practical jokes.

This behaviour first starts the night Anna comes to sleep over.

Unknown to me, Dad sneaks into my room and puts Doona our cat on the spare bed. Doona loves sleeping on beds. What cat doesn't?

Next Dad unwraps a little package that he has bought at the magic shop.

Do you know what is in it? Can you believe this? It is a little piece of brown plastic cat poo. Pretend cat poo. Anyway, he puts this piece of cat poo on Anna's pillow and pulls up the blankets. Then he tiptoes out and closes the door.

I do not know any of this is happening. Anna and I are sitting up late watching videos. We eat chips covered in sauce and drink two whole bottles of Diet Coke.

Finally we decide to go to bed. Anna takes ages and ages cleaning her teeth. She is one of those kids who is right into health. She has a thing about germs. She always places paper on the toilet seat before she sits down. She is *so* clean.

Anyway, she puts on her tracky daks and gets ready for bed. Then she pulls back the blankets. Suddenly she sees the bit of plastic cat poo. 'Ooh, ooh, ooh,' she screams. 'Oh look, disgusting. Foul. Look what the cat's done on my pillow.'

Suddenly Dad bursts into the room. 'What's up, girls?' he says with a silly grin on his face. 'What's all the fuss about?'

Anna is pulling a terrible face. 'Look,' she says in horror as she points at the pillow.

Dad goes over and examines the plastic poo. 'Don't let a little thing like that worry you,' he says. He picks up the plastic poo and pops it into his mouth. He gives a grin. 'D'licioush,' he says through clenched teeth.

'Aargh,' screams Anna. She rushes over to the window and throws up chips, sauce and Diet Coke. Then she looks at Dad in disgust.

Dad is a bit taken aback at Anna being sick. 'It's okay,' he says, taking the plastic poo out of his mouth. 'It's not real.' Dad gives a laugh and off he goes. And off goes Anna. She decides that she wants to go home to her own house. And I don't blame her.

'Dad,' I yell after Anna is gone. 'I am never speaking to you again.'

'Don't be such a sook,' he says. 'It's only a little joke.'

It's always the same. Whenever a friend comes over to stay Dad plays practical jokes. We have fake hands in the rubbish, exploding drinks, pepper in the food, short-sheeted beds and Dracula's blood seeping out of Dad's mouth. Some of the kids think it's great. They wish their Dad was like it.

But I hate it. I just wish he was normal.

He plays tricks on Bianca.

And Yasmin.

And Nga.

And Karla.

None of them go home like Anna. But each time I am so embarrassed.

And now I am worried.

Cynthia is coming to stay. She is the school captain. She is beautiful. She is smart. Everyone wants to be her friend. And now she is sleeping over at our house.

'Dad,' I say. 'No practical jokes. Cynthia is very mature. Her father would never play practical jokes. She might not understand.'

'No worries,' says Dad.

Cynthia arrives but we do not watch videos. We slave away on our English homework. We plan our speeches for the debate in the morning. We go over our parts in the school play. After all that we go out and practise shooting goals because Cynthia is captain of the netball team. Every now and then I pop into the bedroom to check for practical jokes. It is best to be on the safe side.

We also do the washing-up because Cynthia offers – yes *offers* – to do it.

Finally it is time for bed. Cynthia changes into her nightie in the bathroom and then joins me in the bedroom. 'The cat's on my bed,' she says. 'But it doesn't matter. I like cats.' She pulls back the blankets.

And screams. 'Aargh. Cat poo. Filthy cat poo on my pillow.' She yells and yells and yells.

Just then Dad bursts into the room with a silly grin on his face. He goes over and looks at the brown object on the pillow. 'Don't let a little thing like that worry you,' he says. He picks it up and pops it into his mouth. But this time he does not give a grin. His face freezes over.

'Are you looking for this?' I say.

I hold up the bit of plastic poo that Dad had hidden under the blankets earlier that night.

Dad looks at the cat.

Then he rushes over to the window and is sick.

Cynthia and I laugh like mad.

We do love a good joke.

LISTEN EAR

Tell one lie to your parents and you are history. One little fib and they won't ever believe you again.

1

'Brad,' said Dad, 'Never, ever, ever touch this.' In his hand he had the most fantastic compass you have ever seen. Not the type that shows you where to go. The sort you draw circles with.

It was silver and had little metal bolts and a point as sharp as a needle. Instead of a pencil it had a little piece of lead held in by a tiny screw. I whistled. 'Wow,' I said. 'I bet it's worth a fortune.'

'It is,' said Dad. 'And I need it for my work. SO DON'T TOUCH IT.' He put it in the top drawer of the dressing-table in his bedroom and shut it before I could even get a good look.

Geeze, I longed for that compass. Just to hold it, I

mean. Not to steal it or use it or anything like that. Just hold it. That's all I wanted to do.

That compass called to me. 'Brad,' I could hear it saying, 'come and get me. Aren't I great? Pick me up. Look at me. Try me out.'

It didn't really say that. But in my mind it did. All I wanted was a hold. One mingy little hold.

After tea, Mum and Dad and my little sister Sophie went into the lounge to watch TV. It was my turn to do the dishes. Rats. I hate doing the dishes. It is so boring.

'Come and hold me,' called the compass. 'Brad, Brad, Brad.'

I had to go. I just had to. All I wanted was a look. That's all. Just a look. With the tea-towel still in my hand I crept up the stairs. 'Click', I turned on the bedroom light. Softly, softly I tiptoed across the room. Gently, gently I pulled open the drawer. There it was. Dad's compass in all its glory. It sparkled. It twinkled. It was great.

'Pick me up,' it called. 'Pick me up. Just once.' I rubbed my glasses with a dirty finger and stared down at the compass.

It was more than flesh and blood could stand. I put the tea-towel down on the floor and picked up the compass with trembling fingers. It was much heavier than I expected. I opened it up and pretended to draw a little circle in the air.

Just then I heard a sort of scuffling noise. It was almost as if someone was watching. Oh no. Dad would kill me if he caught me with the compass. I dropped the compass into the drawer. Then I turned and ran.

As it turned out no one was coming. Mum and Dad

and Sophie were still watching TV. Maybe the noise was a rat or something.

I walked into the lounge and sat down with the others. 'Bedtime,' said Mum. 'I'll finish the dishes.'

I snuggled down into bed. Something was wrong. The compass was going to cause trouble. I just knew it was. I couldn't get to sleep no matter how hard I tried. I always seem to break things. I mean it isn't my fault. Mostly it is bad luck.

But parents don't understand about accidents. They still think it's your fault. That's why Dad didn't want me to touch the compass. But what could go wrong? I mean I didn't break the compass, did I? It was safely back in the drawer.

I tossed and turned for a couple of hours until something terrible made me jump up. A yell filled the air. It was Dad. I could hear every word even though he was upstairs. 'The compass,' he screamed. 'It's gone.' I could hear footsteps coming my way quickly. I closed my eyes and pretended to be asleep. Maybe they would leave me alone until morning.

Fat chance. Dad ripped the covers back off the bed. 'Don't try that one,' he said. 'I know you're awake.' Boy was he mad.

'Brad,' he said. 'This time you've really gone too far. Where's my compass?'

'I don't know,' I said truthfully. 'I haven't touched it. Sophie must have taken it.'

'Sophie would never take it,' said Mum.

'Neither would I,' I said.

Mum and Dad both looked at me in silence. I knew they were remembering all the bad things I had done.

Like eating Sophie's chocolate Easter bunny one night. Well, she didn't want it. It was five months old and starting to turn white. You know what it's like. You just start by nibbling a tiny bit off the ear where it won't be noticed. Then, before you can blink, the whole ear has gone. So then you might as well scoff the lot because you are going to get caught anyway.

'Did you go in our bedroom?' said Mum.

'No,' I said.

'Did you open the drawer?' asked Dad.

'No,' I answered.

'The drawer was open when we went up to bed,' said Dad.

They both looked at me with cold eyes. I felt sick in my stomach. I must have forgotten to close the drawer.

'And you didn't go into our room?' Mum asked again.

'No,' I said. I know I shouldn't have lied but someone stole the compass and it wasn't me. I didn't want to get the blame for something I didn't do.

'Well,' said Mum, 'if you didn't go into the room how come this was there?' She held up the wet tea-towel that I had been using to dry the dishes. I suddenly went cold all over. Now they would never believe that I hadn't taken the compass.

Well, talk about trouble. They went on and on and on. They wouldn't believe me. Just because I told one little lie. I was grounded until the compass was returned. They wouldn't even let me go to the movies with them the next night. Even though they had promised to take me. And the worst of it was that Sophie got to go. And it must have been her who took the compass.

That's how I happened to be home on my own. Late at night.

2

'The baby-sitter will be here in half an hour,' said Mum.

'I don't need a baby-sitter,' I said. 'I'm not scared. And anyway, she just sits on the phone talking to her boyfriend all night.'

'Where does he live?' said Dad. He was always worried about people making long-distance calls.

'Darwin,' I said.

'He does not,' said Mum. 'He lives right here in Melbourne.'

Dad looked at me with a bit of a smile but he soon lost it when Mum opened up. 'Brad, I really thought you'd have learned not to tell lies by now,' she said.

'It was just a joke,' I said.

The three of them hurried out to the car and drove off.

I locked the front door and stared out of the window. It was growing dark. And it was raining. The clock ticked loudly in the hall. It felt as if I was the only person in the world. I started to feel sorry for myself. It wasn't fair. Okay, I did tell a couple of porkies but I didn't steal the compass. I really wanted to go to the movies and now I was being punished for something I didn't do.

I went over and looked at my face in the lounge-room mirror. My reflection stared back at me. My face looked mean. I just stared and stared into my own eyes. Suddenly

I got the creeps. It was as if the reflection wasn't me. As if it was someone else. I gave a shiver and turned on the television.

Where was that baby-sitter? She should be here by now. Outside it was black and cold. I tried to watch the television but my mind just wasn't on it.

Boomp, scroffle, scraffle. What was that? A sound upstairs. Rats. The rats were in the roof again. Or were they? A little shiver ran down my neck.

Maybe the baby-sitter had crashed her car. I decided to ring up and see if she was okay. June, that was her name. But what was her other name? Dalton. That was it. June Dalton.

Suddenly something terrible happened. The picture on the television zapped itself into a tiny square and disappeared. At the same time the lights went out. Oh no. A power failure. The lines were down again.

I ran to the phone. Nothing. Just a low whistling noise coming down the line.

The house was silent. Where was the baby-sitter? I knew deep inside that she wasn't coming. It was going to be a long night.

Boomp, scroffle, scraffle. There was that noise again. This time from downstairs. Rats. Of course it was rats. No one would want to get in and get me. Would they? The hairs started to stand up on the back of my neck.

There was only one thing to do. Go to bed and fall asleep as quickly as possible. I couldn't spend all night in the dark scared out of my wits. I felt my way along the hall and into my bedroom.

I pulled off my shoes, took off my glasses and jumped

into bed with my clothes on. Then I closed my eyes and tried to sleep. But sleep wouldn't come.

3

So here I am, surrounded by the sounds of the night.

Houses make a lot of noise when you are the only person in them. Squeak. Creak. Rustle. Rumble. What was that? Nothing. Don't be silly. You are alone. Aren't you?

Who would want to get you? Just a boy. Just an ordinary boy. Okay, so I told a couple of lies. But I'm not really mean. I don't deserve to die. I'm quite a nice person really.

What if there was someone under the bed? What if a hand slowly started to pull the blankets down. Until I was uncovered? A horrible cold hand with grey fingers. Go away. Go away if you are there. Leave me alone. I won't tell any more lies, God. I promise. And I'll do the washing-up on my own. Every night.

Well, nearly every night.

Where did that shadow in the corner come from? It looks like a man with a hat. Standing. Staring. Who's that breathing so loudly?

Me, of course.

Only me. I am alone. I hope. I try to breathe softly. Just in case there is someone creeping around looking for me. They won't know where I am. Unless I make a noise.

The room starts to become lighter. It's funny that – how you can see better in the dark after a while. It is not a man in the corner. It is just my dressing-gown hanging on a hook.

But what is that lump on the wall? That wasn't there yesterday. A small bump in the plaster. It must be my imagination. I can't see a thing without my glasses. I reach out and put them on. Then I take another look. Yes, it is a lump on the wall. Where did that come from? It looks like a table-tennis ball half buried in the wall. I stare and stare at it.

It's weird how your mind plays tricks on you. I could swear that the lump is bigger than before. I could swear that it is growing.

Aaaaaaaaargh. It is growing. I can see it wobbling and moving. I can't take my eyes off it. I am hypnotised by it. A horrible, swelling growth on the wall.

'Mum,' I want to scream. But I am too frightened. The word is frozen in my throat.

I am trembling with fear. I am too scared to run. And too scared to stay. Help. Help. Someone. Anyone. Please. Make the lump go away. Come and save me.

I need help.

It is wiggling. The ear is wiggling.

The ear?

Yes. Oh horrible, horrible, horrible. The lump is in the shape of an ear. A wiggling, disgusting, plaster ear on the wall. It is listening. Listening. Listening.

It is the ear of the house. I bet it heard me tell Mum lies. It is the ear that hears all. Knows all. Understands all. Sneaky. Snaky. Snoopy. It is looking for liars.

Well, listen, ear. Just see what you think of this. I take a deep breath. I fill up my lungs. I am terrified but I must be brave. I yell as loud as I can.

'Nick off, ear.'

The sound echoes around the empty rooms. But the ear does not nick off. It just wiggles a little bit. Like a worm on the end of a hook.

4

All is silent again. Tick, tick, tick. Rustle, rustle. Breathe in. Breathe out. Silently. Quiet.

Wiggle, wiggle. There it goes again. Don't annoy it. Don't shout. Don't even look. Pretend it is not there.

The ghastly ear on the wall.

Oh, oh, oh. No. It isn't. Not another lump. It can't be. I sneak a look through half-closed eyelids. Another foul lump is swelling out of the plaster. Yes, oh yuck. Another ear. A pair of ears wiggling on the wall. Stop, stop, stop.

Be a dream. Be a nightmare. Don't be real. Please don't be real.

I look at the wall. But the ears are still there. This is not a dream. This is real. The ears are still there in the wall. One of them has an earring. Just like mine but made of plaster. The ears are living, wriggling plaster.

There is more movement. It is as if the plaster is growing a mole. Or bubbling like thick soup in a dark pot. Bits are boiling and growing.

Oh, what's this? A nose. And eyes. And a chin. A face grows like a flower opening on fast forward.

A face in the wall. The plaster eyes roll around. The nose twitches. The mouth opens and closes but it says nothing. It is like the television with the sound turned down. The eyes stare at me. They see me hiding there under the covers, trying not to look.

I have seen this face before. But where? Whose face is this?

What can I do? I can't stay here with the fiendish face. I will run for it. Down to the kitchen. I will wait in the kitchen until Mum and Dad come home.

The face is still boiling and bubbling. What? It has grown glasses. They are just like mine but made of plaster.

I stare at the face. It stares back at me. Blinking with plaster eyes.

I know where I have seen this face before. I have seen it in the mirror.

It is my face.

I scream. I jump out of bed. I race along to the kitchen and slam the door. I fall panting to the floor. I am never going in that bedroom again.

Oh Dad, Mum, Sophie, baby-sitter. Where are you? Come home, come home, come home.

I can't bear to look at the walls. Or go near them. So I sit on the floor with my back against the fridge. It is cold on the tile floor but I am going to stay there until someone comes home.

I lean my head back on the fridge door and close my eyes. The metal is cold and hard against my head. And it is moving. Like worms crawling in my hair. For a moment I just sit there, frozen. Then I scream and scramble across the floor.

The face has erupted in the door of the fridge. Only now it is a horrible, horrible steel face with shiny white skin and lips and eyes. Its glasses are also white steel.

50

The face, my face is trying to talk. Its lips are moving but nothing is coming out. What is it trying to say?

It is me. I know that it is me. It is my own conscience. Telling me not to tell lies.

'Leave me alone,' I scream. 'Leave me alone.' I bolt into the lounge and crouch behind the sofa.

But it has followed me.

There it is on the window. Now the face is made of glass. I can see right through its dreadful, moving lips. Is it calling me a liar? What is it trying to say? What is it doing? Why is it after me? Why? Why? Why?

I jump up and roar out of the room. I am running away from myself. No one can do that.

5

I bolt into Dad's study. The walls are all made of wood. The face can't get me here. I am safe.

Outside the rain has stopped. The moon is playing hide and seek behind the clouds. How I wish I was on the moon. I stare up but then look away. Even the moon has a face.

The moonlight shines on the dark wooden panels. The grain makes strange shapes like whirlpools in a rotting swamp. The lines begin to swirl and run like a crazy river.

My heart starts to beat faster and faster. I can feel the blood running beneath my skin. Sheer terror is washing within me.

The fearsome face has made itself in a panel. My awful reflection glares down at me through its wooden glasses.

Its mouth opens and shuts without a sound. It is trying to say something. But what?

It is no use running. The face can turn itself into plaster and steel and glass. And wood. There is no escape.

A saying that I once heard is stirring in the back of my mind. What is it? I know. 'The best form of defence is attack.'

Could I attack the face? It might grab me and pull me into the wall. Never to be seen again. But I can't keep running. If I go outside it might appear on a tree. Or the footpath. There is nowhere to run. Nowhere to go. No escape.

I must beat it at its own game. Think, think, think. What is its weakness? It is my face. How can I outsmart it?

I am breathing so heavily that my glasses start to fog up. I give them a wipe. I can't see a thing without my glasses. If I lose them I am gone.

The face still mouths silent words. And peers at me through its wooden glasses.

Okay. It is risky. It is a chance. But I have to take it. On hands and knees I crawl towards the grained face in the wood. Behind the sofa. Along. I must keep my head down. I must get close without it knowing what I am up to.

I crouch low behind the sofa like a cat waiting for a bird. I can't see the face and it can't see me. Unless it has moved.

Now. Go, go, go.

I fly at the face like an arrow from a bow.

Snatch. Got them. Got them. I can't believe it. I have

grabbed the wooden glasses. The face is horrified. Its mouth opens in a silent scream. Its eyes are wide and staring. It rushes blindly around the walls. Like a rat running under a sheet it shoots across the floor.

Its features change as it rushes to and fro. Glass, wood, plastic. It bubbles across the floor. Searching, searching, searching. Its mouth snaps and snarls. Its eyes gape and glare but without the glasses it cannot see. Oh, what will it do if it catches me?

Flash. A blinding light fills the room. What? I blink in the glare. Oh yes, yes, yes. The power has come back on. I have light. Now maybe the fiendish face will go back where it came from.

But no. In the light it is more fearsome than ever. More real. I am so scared. My knees are shaking so much that I can hardly move.

Suddenly from the lounge-room I hear – voices. A woman's voice. And a child's. They are home. 'Mum,' I scream. 'Mum, Mum, Mum.' I race into the hall towards the lounge and the face follows my voice. But I don't care. They are here. Help has arrived. I am saved.

I rush into the lounge and then freeze. There are people there all right. But they won't be any use to me. They are on the television. The television has come back on with the power. It is my favourite show – 'Round the Twist'.

6

I run out of the room and up the stairs. The face follows the sound of my thumping feet. Now it is made of carpet.

A carpet face flowing up the stairs after my footsteps.

I run into Mum and Dad's room and slam the door.

Fool. Fool. What a mistake. The face heard the door slam. It bulges out onto the door. Staring. Searching. It knows I am in the room. I climb carefully onto the bed and try to breathe quietly. It can't find me. Not without the glasses. Not unless I make a noise. Don't move. Don't make the bed squeak.

The face starts to search. Up and down each wall. Across the ceiling. Under the bed. Its lips are pulled down in an unhappy pout. It circles the bed like a shark around a boat. It knows where I am.

'Listen,' I yell. 'I am sorry I told a lie. I'm sorry, sorry, sorry. Okay?'

This is weird. I am telling myself that I am sorry.

The face suddenly smiles. It is happy. Its mouth is making silent words. What is it trying to say? One word. It is saying the same word over and over again.

It is hard reading lips. But suddenly I know what the word is.

'Glasses,' I yell at the face.

The face nods. Up and down with a limp smile.

What is it about these glasses? I take my own glasses off and carefully put the wooden ones on my own face. Straight away everything changes. The whole house is different. I can see through the walls and the ceiling. The house is a ghost house and I can see right through it.

Wires and building materials. Nails. Rubbish. An old newspaper. A drink bottle left by the builders. A rat's nest underneath the dressing-table. A rat scurries away through a hole in the wall.

This is amazing. I can see into all the rooms from where I am standing. It is like X-ray vision.

My mind starts to turn over. Somewhere in all this is the answer to a puzzle. The rat's nest. I stare and stare at the rat's nest. All of this started with rats scuttling around in the wall. I stare into the nest. Then I smile.

So does the face. It is happy too.

I do not know if the face is my conscience. Perhaps it is the best and the worst of me. It has chased me around and made me feel guilty. And now it has helped me out.

I step down from the bed. I walk over to the grinning copy of myself and put the glasses on its cheeks. It blinks. 'Thank you,' I say. 'You can go now.'

Slowly, slowly with just the hint of a smile, the face melts back into the wall. I know that it is happy.

Downstairs a door bangs. 'Mum,' I yell. 'Dad. Sophie.' I rush happily down the stairs.

'The baby-sitter rang the cinema,' says Mum. 'Her car broke down. And the phones weren't working. Are you okay?'

'Sit down,' I say. 'You are not going to believe this.'

They sit down and don't say a thing while I tell them the story. I tell them everything and don't leave out one little detail.

I am right about one thing though. They do not believe me.

'It was a dream,' says Mum.

'It was a lie,' says Dad.

They think I am still lying. They won't believe me. 'It's the truth,' I yell. 'It is, it is, it is.'

'There is one way to prove your story,' says Dad. 'We

will move the dressing-table and see if there is a rat's nest underneath. Then we will know for sure.'

We all walk up to the bedroom and Dad tries to move the dressing-table. It is very heavy so the whole four of us join in and help. In the end we lift it into the middle of the room.

There against the wall is a rat's nest. There is no rat in it. It has run away because of all the noise. There is no rat. But there is a compass. Right there where the rat carried it.

'Now do you believe me?' I say.

I look at Mum and Dad and Sophie. Their mouths just open and shut but no sound comes out.

No sound at all.

PICKED BONES

Uncle Sam's dead body.

I can sort of picture it in my mind.

He is stretched out on the desert sand. Wild animals have torn his clothes. Birds have pecked at him. There is nothing left except his skeleton.

And the box – clutched in the bones of one hand. And a rusty nail clasped in the other.

1

Poor Uncle Sam. It was a horrible way to die. All alone in the outback with no friends. And no one knowing what happened.

Uncle Sam was a birdwatcher. He loved native birds and he hated feral cats. 'They get out in the outback and breed,' he used to say. 'They don't belong in this country.

The birds have no defences. One cat will eat over a hundred birds a year.'

Uncle Sam had done a lot for the native wildlife in Australia. But now he was gone. Dad arranged for the bones to be brought back and we had a funeral. I watched sadly as the coffin went down into the grave. We were alike were Uncle Sam and I. Two greenies trying to save the world. And now he was gone. It was the saddest thing ever.

As we walked out of the cemetery Dad wiped his wet eyes and handed me the box. It was made of carved wood and on the top was scratched: FOR TERRY. KEEP AWAY FROM K . . . The writing trailed off. Uncle Sam must have died while he was scratching the message with the nail.

'What's in it?' I asked Dad.

'I don't know,' he said. 'It doesn't have a lid. Anyway, I wouldn't open a present with someone else's name on it. It was meant for you.'

That's the sort of guy Dad is. He wouldn't even read your diary if it was left open on the desk. Still, he looked worried. 'Uncle Sam was a bit weird,' he said. 'Heaven knows what's in that box. You be careful with it.'

After the funeral everyone came back to our house for the wake. There was lots of drinking and laughing. It didn't seem right to me. 'Why is everyone having a good time?' I said to Mum.

She looked at me and smiled. 'Uncle Sam would have wanted it,' she said. 'We've said goodbye to him at the graveyard. That was the time to cry. Now we have to get on with life. That's the way it is.'

I still didn't like it. I went up to my room and shut the door so I couldn't hear all the noise. I put the box on my bed and had a good look at it. The wood had steel bands around it. There was no lid and no keyhole. I would have to get a saw to cut it open. But I didn't want to do that. It was too good. And I might break what was in it.

It was sort of spooky to look at the scratched writing on the lid. The last words of Uncle Sam. Written to me – his best mate. He died at the very moment of scratching out these letters. I shivered and put the box under my bed. Then I went down to join the party.

By now everyone had had too much to drink. They were drowning their sorrows. Laughing and arguing and telling jokes and stories. Mum was even speaking to Aunt Marjory. I couldn't believe it.

They hadn't spoken to each other since Aunt Marjory gave me Knuckles for Christmas. Mum had to let me keep Knuckles seeing that he was a Christmas present. She said that Aunt Marjory only gave him to me because he was a horrible cat and she wanted to get rid of him. Pet cats are okay if you keep them away from the native animals. But Knuckles was mean and sneaky. He yowled and scowled. He spat and hissed. He scratched our sofa to pieces. He wouldn't let anyone touch him. He was the king of the neighbourhood. All the other cats disappeared when Knuckles was around. And I just couldn't keep him in at night. He would always manage to get out and go hunting for birds.

Knuckles was my only pet. I *used* to have guinea pigs – two cute little black and white ones. Until Knuckles got into their cage one night and ate them both for supper. Now I had no pets except Knuckles. Not that you could call Knuckles a pet. A crocodile would have been more fun.

That got me to thinking. Knuckles. Where was he? Nowhere to be seen. That was strange. Normally he would be up on the table licking the best food. Then no one would eat anything and I would be in trouble for letting him inside.

I prowled around the house hunting for Knuckles. I looked in the kitchen. Under the tables. Behind the fridge. In the laundry basket. All the usual places. But he was nowhere to be seen.

I went upstairs to my room and caught sight of something strange. Through the window. Outside. On the porch roof. Knuckles was standing there. And when I say standing that's what I mean. Standing on his two back legs. And flapping his front ones up and down like chicken wings. He was staring into my bedroom window and waving his front legs about like a crazy chook.

2

Something strange was going on. Something really weird. There was Knuckles. Outside. On the window ledge trying to get in. He was screeching and yowling something terrible. He clawed at the glass with vicious swipes. I tapped on the window. 'Buzz off,' I said. 'You're not getting in until dark. No way.'

Suddenly, as if a clever thought had just crossed his

mind, Knuckles turned and jumped down to the ground.

I picked up the box and examined it. What was inside? And how could I open it?

I gave the box a gentle shake and held my ear up to it. Nothing. Not a murmur. This was driving me crazy. What could be inside? I read the scratched words again. KEEP AWAY FROM K . . .

Something was wrong. I could feel it in my bones. I thought about that last word that Uncle Sam had been scratching on the lid. KEEP AWAY FROM K . . . He had been about to scratch a word starting with 'k' when he died. There were lots of possibilities. Kangaroos. Kookaburras. Kids. I looked around the room. There was a bunch of keys on my shelf. It could even be them. Just to be on the safe side I picked them up and threw them into the hallway.

I made one final check and couldn't see anything else that started with 'k'. I wasn't too good at spelling but I thought I had found everything. There was nothing left starting with 'k'. All I needed now was a saw.

Suddenly I felt nervous. There could be something dangerous inside. Maybe I should go and ask Dad to saw the box open.

Downstairs the party was getting louder and louder. I looked out of the window. People were staggering around out on the back lawn. Uncle Russell was having a pee behind some bushes. Another group were arguing about whether the women should have been allowed to carry Uncle Sam's coffin. Mum was saying they should. 'Women are not strong enough,' I heard Aunt Marjory say.

'Don't be ridiculous,' said Mum. 'It's not as if he weighed much. He was only bones.'

They were all off their faces. No, none of the adults would help.

I stared at the box. So did Knuckles.

Knuckles.

He was inside the house. He was inside my room. He had sneaked in while the drunken mourners were going in and out. Knuckles had a strange look in his eyes. A wild but gentle look. He pounced over to the box and started purring. Purring, do you mind. Knuckles had never purred in his life. He looked like a cat that had just eaten the cream. Knuckles was purring at the box.

He was staring at the box and licking his lips. It almost looked as if he was reading the writing on the lid. Uncle Sam's last words so to speak. KEEP AWAY FROM K . . . Of course. That was it. Why didn't I see it before? KEEP AWAY FROM KNUCKLES.

I mustn't let Knuckles get near the box. Whatever was inside could be damaged by cats. Even now Knuckles' very presence could be ruining something valuable. It could be treasure of some sort. Melting away because a cat was in the room.

'Get out,' I yelled. 'Go on. Buzz off, Knuckles.' I had to shoo him out before he ruined everything.

Knuckles turned around slowly. He crouched down and the fur on his neck stood up like a necklace made of poisoned needles. His eyes were filled with hate. His muscles quivered, ready to spring. I had never seen an animal with such a vicious look in its eyes. I don't mind telling you I was scared. Scared of a cat.

'Okay,' I said, 'okay. Take it easy, Knuckles.' I took a few steps backwards to show that I meant no harm.

Knuckles relaxed and turned back to the box. Then he did something weird. He started licking the box. Licking and purring at the same time.

Amazing. A cat licking a wooden box. It was strange. But not as strange as what happened next.

Click. The lid of the box sprang open.

Imagine that. Knuckles' spit had released the catch. Crazy but true. Now I could find out what was inside. I was dying to know. I took a silent step forward.

Hiss, spit, hiss. Knuckles crouched low, hate in his eyes. I backed slowly away. 'All right, all right,' I said. 'Don't go off your brain.'

Knuckles relaxed. Then he suddenly leapt. Not at me. Not at anyone. He jumped onto the top of the open box and curled up. Straight away he began to purr. He reminded me of a dragon curled up on its pile of jewels and gold.

What was inside the box? What was it? I just had to know. I couldn't handle this on my own. Knuckles might ruin everything. KEEP AWAY FROM KNUCKLES. That's what Uncle Sam had been writing. It was time to bring in the big guns. I went off to get the adults.

3

Most of the guests had called taxis and gone home. Their cars were still parked in the drive. They would probably come back and get them in the morning. When they felt a little better, if you know what I mean. Anyway, Dad and Mum and Aunt Marjory were still there. So was Uncle

Russell. They all stared into my bedroom. Knuckles was still curled up on the box. Purring.

'He's a lovely cat,' said Aunt Marjory. 'He just loves me, you know.'

'Why did you give him to Terry then?' said Mum.

'A sacrifice,' said Aunt Marjory. 'I had to make the sacrifice. All children need a pet.'

'He won't get off the box,' I said. 'Knuckles isn't allowed near the box. I can't get him off. He's the meanest cat in the world.'

'Nonsense,' said Aunt Marjory. 'He's as quiet as a lamb.' She walked over and bent down to pick up Knuckles.

Swish. Swipe. Snarl. Knuckles struck out. Quicker than a snake's tongue.

'Aargh.' Aunt Marjory fell back with a terrible scream. Thin red lines of blood ran across her face. Aunt Marjory scrambled to her feet and ran into the corridor. She rushed to the hall mirror. 'My face,' she yelled. 'My beautiful face.'

Uncle Russell tried not to laugh at that.

Aunt Marjory looked at me in fury. 'You've ruined that cat,' she yelled. 'He had a beautiful nature before.'

'Perhaps you'd like him back,' said Mum.

'Now, now girls,' said Uncle Russell. 'No need to argue. I'll get the cat. I'm good with animals.'

He was brave, was Uncle Russell. There's no doubt about that. Raw Australian courage. He had heaps of it. He just strode across the room and grabbed the cat. Just like that. Bent down and picked up Knuckles by the scruff of the neck.

64

And just like that Knuckles twisted out of his hands. And fixed himself to Uncle Russell's face. Knuckles was so quick you could hardly see him move. He wrapped his legs around Uncle Russell's head. Uncle Russell's face was buried in Knuckles' trembling body.

'Mmff, ggg, mnnff.' Uncle Russell fell onto the bed. We couldn't hear what he was trying to say. He couldn't speak. He couldn't breathe. He was suffocating. Knuckles was killing Uncle Russell. He pulled and pulled at Knuckles but the horrible animal had its claws sunk into his neck.

'Quick,' screamed Dad. 'Turn on the shower, Terry.'

The shower? This was no time for a shower.

Dad started to lead Uncle Russell out into the corridor. The cat still clung to his head.

Mum ran into the bathroom and turned on the shower.

'Oh,' said Aunt Marjory. 'Oh, oh, oh. What have you done to that cat?'

Dad took Uncle Russell into the bathroom. He looked like a man wearing a hairy blindfold. Dad pushed his head under the cold water. Knuckles dropped off, wet and bedraggled. Uncle Russell collapsed onto the floor, gasping for air.

Knuckles sped back towards the bedroom.

'Quick, Terry,' shouted Dad. 'Shut the door. Don't let him back in.'

I wanted to shut the door. I mean I meant to shut the door. I was just a bit slow that's all. I wanted to see what was in the box. I had to know. I just managed to get a glimpse. Then I ran for the door. Too late. Knuckles flashed by. Straight back onto the box.

Uncle Russell wiped the blood off his neck. 'Right,' he said. 'That cat is history.'

'I know what's in the box,' I said.

They all fell silent and looked at me.

'Well?' said Mum.

'Eggs,' I said. 'Two lovely bird's eggs.'

4

We all stared through the doorway at Knuckles. He was curled up on the box, purring and looking happy. In an evil sort of way.

'Isn't he sweet?' said Aunt Marjory. 'He thinks he's their mother. He's trying to hatch the eggs.'

She was right. And she was wrong. He was trying to hatch the eggs. But he didn't think he was their mother. I didn't think so anyway. Not for one minute. Knuckles licked his lips.

'He's going to eat them,' I screamed. 'Knuckles is going to hatch the eggs and then eat the birds. That's why Uncle Sam scratched "Keep Away From K . . ." on the lid. Keep away from Knuckles. Uncle Sam knew I had a pet cat.'

I could just see it in my mind. Two lovely little birds. Helpless. Harmless. Newborn chicks. Knuckles would eat them alive.

'He's right,' said Dad. 'And we don't know what sort of birds they are. They could be very rare. We have to save them. That's what Sam would have wanted.'

'And me,' I said. 'That's what I want too.'

Uncle Russell nodded. 'Leave it to me. I'll fix the ruddy cat. No worries.'

'Don't hurt him,' said Aunt Marjory. 'He means well.'

'I'll do it, Russell,' said Dad. 'You can be a bit rash sometimes.'

Dad went out to the backyard and fetched our rubbish bin. You know – the sort with wheels that you get from the council. Dad tipped out the rubbish and cut a small hole in the side. Then he put on a raincoat and slipped a garden glove on one hand.

We took the bin upstairs and Dad hopped inside and closed the lid. He looked out of the hole. 'Wheel me in,' he said. 'Park me next to the box. I'll stick out my gloved hand and grab Knuckles. He won't be able to get at me because I'll be inside the bin. Then you wheel me outside and we dump Knuckles in a cage.'

It was a good plan.

Uncle Russell carefully wheeled the bin into my bedroom. Knuckles hissed and raised his fur but he stayed curled up on the eggs. Uncle Russell quickly walked back to us. He was in a hurry to get out of the way. And I didn't blame him. Not one bit.

We all held our breath and watched. The fingers of Dad's glove slowly moved out of the hole. Then the whole glove. Then Dad's arm, safely enclosed in the raincoat. The glove moved closer and closer to Knuckles. The cat didn't move. Well, only his eyes. Knuckles' eyes were glued to that glove. Dad opened his fingers just above Knuckles' neck. In any second he would have Knuckles firmly by the scruff of the neck.

Peow. Talk about fast. I've never seen anything like it.

Knuckles moved like a flash. His teeth sank into the glove. Into Dad's fingers. 'Ouch,' came Dad's muffled voice from inside. He shook his arm around like a crazy windmill. Knuckles hung on for grim death. A ginger streak, whipping back and forth through the air. 'Et it off, et it off,' came a shrieking voice from inside the bin.

'What did he say?' asked Mum.

'Sounds like "Get it off",' said Uncle Russell.

Before anyone could move, Dad pulled his hand back inside the bin.

The only trouble was, he pulled Knuckles in with it.

There was dead silence for about two seconds. I snatched a look at where the eggs had been. 'Look,' I yelled.

But no one did. A terrible yowling, howling noise came from the bin. Was it Dad? Or was it Knuckles? You couldn't tell. The screeching and shaking went on and on and on. Something horrible was going on in there. The bin rocked and rolled. Hissed and heaved. There was a lot of pain inside that bin.

'Don't hurt Knuckles,' yelled Aunt Marjory. 'He means well.'

Suddenly a silence fell over the room. The bin stopped shaking. A bleeding and tattered glove pushed up the lid. 'I surrender,' came Dad's voice. With a quick yowl, Knuckles flashed out of the bin and sat back on his perch. He licked his lips and started to purr.

Slowly, slowly Dad emerged from the bin. Like a long-buried corpse rising from the grave. He was scratched, torn and bleeding. His clothes shredded to rags. It was a terrible sight. He didn't have enough strength to get out

of the bin. Uncle Russell had to wheel him down the stairs
into the kitchen.

5

Altogether Mum put thirty-five bandaids on Dad. He was
scratched from head to toe.

'At at as oo go,' said Dad. He could hardly move his
bleeding lips.

'What?' said Aunt Marjory.

'That cat has to go,' said Mum.

'It does too,' I said. 'The eggs have hatched.'

They all looked at me.

I took a deep breath. 'They're funny looking birds with
no feathers and great big beaks. And ...'

'Yes?' said Uncle Russell.

'Nothing,' I said. I was too embarrassed to say. In case
I was wrong. I mean I only had a quick look.

'I've got an idea,' said Mum. 'We'll put some cat food
on a saucer outside the door. As soon as Knuckles comes
out to get it, Russell can nip inside the room and lock
him out.'

'I dunno,' said Uncle Russell. 'He moves pretty fast.'

'I'll do it,' I said. 'I have to save those birds. They could
be the last of the species. Uncle Sam put his trust in me.'

'No,' said Uncle Russell. 'I'll do it.'

Mum put two lamb chops on a saucer and placed them
on the floor outside my door. Knuckles looked up and
sniffed. Quick as a whippet he flashed over to the saucer
and grabbed the meat.

None of us moved. We forgot all about shutting the door. We were too busy gawking at the birds. They had already grown feathers. Their beaks were enormous. They were squawking for food.

Knuckles grabbed the raw chops. But he didn't eat them. He turned round and gave one each to the birds. They gobbled them down like crazy. Knuckles just stood and watched. It was like he was in a trance. Or a spell. Soon only the chop bones were left. Picked clean.

'Isn't he kind?' said Aunt Marjory.

'He's fattening them up,' I said. 'To eat. Like in *Hansel and Gretel.*'

The birds screeched and chirped for more. They looked at Knuckles, standing there as if he was hypnotised.

We just stared at those birds. None of us had ever seen birds like them before. My eyes hadn't tricked me. I really had seen what I thought I'd seen. They had teeth. Birds with teeth. Can you imagine that?

Dad closed the door. We all felt uneasy. I pressed my ear to the wall.

A terrible screeching, squealing, chirping and burping came from inside. 'Oh no,' I yelled. 'Knuckles is eating the birds.'

We all rushed downstairs and out the door. Uncle Russell scrambled up a vine onto the porch roof and peered in the window. 'Horrible,' he mumbled. 'Just horrible.'

We all climbed up after him. There wasn't much room on the porch roof by the time we were all perched up there. We stared inside. The birds sat on the end of my bed, wiping their teeth on my sheets. Knuckles was nowhere to be seen.

Suddenly it clicked. We all realised at the same time. KEEP AWAY FROM KNUCKLES. That was the message. But it wasn't to stop Knuckles eating the birds. It was to stop the . . .

Knuckles lay stretched out on the floor. All that was left of him. There was nothing but bones. A skeleton, totally picked clean.

6

It was time for a council of war. Dad nailed up my bedroom door and we all sat around the kitchen table.

'Sam must have bred them,' said Dad, 'to even things up. To get rid of feral cats.'

'That's what the message was for,' I said. 'He knew I had a pet cat. He wanted to warn me.'

'It's not right,' yelled Aunt Marjory. 'Birds that eat cats. It's not right.'

'Why not?' I yelled back. 'Feral cats eat birds. What's the difference?'

'Sam hated feral cats,' said Dad. 'He must have bred these birds to give the native animals a chance.'

'To save the environment,' I said.

'What are we going to do with them?' asked Uncle Russell. 'They could be the only two in the world.'

'They're mine,' I said. 'Uncle Sam gave them to me. I'm keeping them.'

'Better call the zoo,' said Mum. 'They'll take them off our hands.'

I didn't want them to go. They were my birds. I loved them. They couldn't help it if they liked cats (so to speak). I wasn't going to let anyone take them away.

Suddenly Aunt Marjory jumped up. She ran outside and grabbed a shovel. 'I'll take them off your hands,' she yelled. 'Murdering mongrels.'

Oh no. She was going to kill the birds. She ran over to the vine and started climbing. I followed as quickly as I could. Aunt Marjory lifted up the shovel and smashed my window before I could stop her. Then she started to climb inside. I tried to pull her back but she was too strong. She clambered into my room. I went in after her.

Where were the birds? They were nowhere to be seen.

There were two lumps under my bed covers. The birds were snuggled down in my bed. Aunt Marjory rushed over and pulled back the covers. The birds were twice as big as before. I have never seen anything like it. They had hatched and become adults in less than a day. The birds looked up with funny smiles that showed their teeth.

No, they weren't smiling at Aunt Marjory. No one would want to eat her. They were smiling at the open window.

Before anyone could move they flapped their wings and flew out into the sunshine. They rose high in the air and circled over the house. Then they headed west into the sunset.

We never saw them again. I was so sad. Uncle Sam had left those birds in my care and now they were gone.

They were cute in their own way, were those birds. Even if they did have teeth.

'Probably gone back to the desert,' said Uncle Russell.

'They'll never make it,' said Aunt Marjory. 'It's a long way. Someone will shoot them.'

I looked at Aunt Marjory. 'You are so mean,' I said. I ran up to my room and shut the door. I was heart-broken.

I jumped into my bed.

I touched something with my toes.

I looked under the covers.

I smiled.

I decided not to tell anyone what I had found.

I put the two freshly laid eggs into Uncle Sam's box and gently closed the lid.

Then I went over to the window and looked out at the rising moon.

It was a lovely summer's evening. I could see a cat on the prowl. Someone had let it out at night. And it was hunting for birds. It turned and looked at the box in my hands. Then it started to walk towards me with a funny expression on its face.

JUST LIKE ME

I love you.

Now that's a thing no self-respecting twelve-year-old would say to a girl.

Well, you couldn't really, could you? Not when she was the most beautiful girl in the class. In the school. In the country. In the whole world. In those days I would have said the whole universe.

A skinny, dorky kid like me couldn't have said it to her.

Here I am, a grown man. Twenty-one years old and my stomach still gets the wobbles when I think about Fay.

Maybe it's because I might see her again. In five minutes or so.

See, we buried a time capsule in the wall of the old school. And Mr Wheeler made us promise to come back exactly nine years later. When all the kids would be twenty-one years old. I feel a bit foolish actually. Probably no one else will turn up. They will have forgotten. I'll be the only idiot there. And I've flown all the way out from England.

I turn my car into Brewer Road. Soon I'll be at the school. Everything looks different. Where did all those office blocks come from?

The old park has gone. And the fish and chip shop. And the pond where we used to catch frogs.

Oh, oh, oh. No. It isn't. It can't be. It must be a mistake. Look what they have done. No, no, no.

The school is not there.

There's a dirty big shopping centre. With a car park and thousands of cars. Signposts. Balloons. Loud speakers. Escalators. Security guards.

They have pulled down the school and the trees and the bike shed. They have pulled down my dreams and built a nightmare.

I park my car and wander in through the huge doors. Jaws, more like it. I ride the escalators to the top of the mall and look down at the fountain far below. There are hundreds of shoppers. People sipping coffee, staring into windows, pushing trolleys, dragging children, carrying parcels.

There is no one digging out a time capsule from a school wall. There is no one from Grade Six at Bentleigh West State School. And even if there was I wouldn't recognise them.

All I have left is memories.

I think back and remember what I wrote when I was twelve. The letter I put in the time capsule. The letter that has gone for ever. That no one will read. The letter I wrote to a girl I will never see again.

Dear Fay,

My Mum and Dad are moving to England. So it looks like I will never see you again. Not till I'm twenty-one, anyway. And that's ancient. Anyway, that's how old you will be when you get this letter. If you are there. When they dig out the time capsule, I mean.

I will be there for sure.

I feel stupid writing this. But no one will know. If Luke Jeffries knew he would give me heaps. So would his nerdy mates. They pick on me. Just because I've got freckles. I hate them, I hate them, I hate them.

My first day at this school was awful. I knew I would cop it. I'm not like you. See, you are the netball captain. You are good at everything. You get A's for every subject. The teachers always pick you to do jobs. They hold up your work out the front.

You are good-looking. No – scrub that. You are better than that. I'll tell you what I think about you. It will be all right because no one will read this until the time capsule is opened.

You are gorgeous. If I was a cat you would be the cream. If I was a dog you would be the bone. If I was a rock you would be the waterfall running over me.

You are the top and I'm the bottom. I'm not any good at anything. Except drawing. Mum says I'm a good drawer.

Anyway, I'm getting off the track. I want to tell you about my first day at school. There I was standing out the front with nowhere to sit. In the end I had to use Mr Wheeler's chair. He said, 'You can sit there for the present.'

Everyone gawked at me. You were the only one who smiled.

When the bell went I stayed on my seat. Mr Wheeler said, 'What are you waiting for, Ben?'

I said, 'I'm waiting for the present.'

Everyone packed up. They all laughed like mad. Except you. My face was burning, I can tell you that. Talk about embarrassing.

After that my problems just got bigger and bigger. I couldn't get out what I was thinking. When they picked on me I couldn't say a thing.

I would like you to be my friend. But you are popular and I'm not.

You sit at the desk in front of me. Your ponytail hangs down and swishes across my books. It is gold like the tail of an angel's horse. I would like to touch it but of course I never would.

My stomach goes all wobbly when I look at you.

I wanted to give you something. But I didn't have any money. Mum is always broke. 'Make something,' she said. 'It's the thought that counts. If you want to give a present make it yourself.'

Well, it was coming up to Easter so I decided to draw on an Easter egg. Seeing as how I am good at drawing.

I got an egg and put a little hole in each end. Then I blew out all the insides and started painting.

Three weeks. That's how long it took. I sat up every night until Mum went crook and made me put out the light. It was going to be the best egg ever in the history of the world. I painted rabbits. And a gnome with a fishing rod. And a heart with your initials on it. All covered in flowers.

Mum reckoned it was a little ripper. 'Ben,' she said. 'That is beautiful. It is the most lovely Easter egg I have ever seen.'

So I wrapped it up in cotton wool and put it in a box.

Then I start to get scared. What if you didn't like it? What if you showed everyone and they laughed? What if *you* laughed?

Oh geeze. I'm scared, Fay. I'm glad you won't get this till I'm twenty-one.

It turned out worse than I thought.

As soon as I walked in the school gate I was in trouble. Luke Jeffries grabbed the box. 'Look at this,' he yelled. 'Ben has a cute little egg for Fay. I wonder why?'

All the kids gave me heaps. They really rubbished me. 'Give it back,' I whispered. My face was burning like an oven.

Luke Jeffries threw the box on the ground. 'This is an egg,' he said. 'So we will hatch it.' He sat down on the box and clucked like a hen. The egg was smashed to bits.

I turned round and went for it. I just ran and ran and ran. I didn't care about wagging school. I didn't care about anything. Except a present for you.

I ran into the kitchen and grabbed another egg. There was no time to blow it out. There was no time to paint rabbits and gnomes and things. I put on some boiling water to hard-boil an egg. Then I tipped in some dye.

And that's when it happened. I was angry and rushing around. I slipped over with the saucepan in my hands. The water sloshed onto my cheeks. Oh, the pain. Oh, my face was burning. Oh, it hurt. I'm not a sook. But I screamed and screamed and screamed.

I didn't remember anything else till I woke up in hospital.

My face still burned. But I couldn't touch it. I was wearing a mask. Bandages. I looked like a robber. There were little holes for my mouth and eyes and nostrils.

'Your face will be okay,' said Mum. 'But you will have to wear the mask for a long time while it heals.'

'I'm not going to school like this. No way.'

'You have to,' said Mum. 'You have to wear the mask for six months or your face won't heal properly.'

So I walked in the classroom late. Looking like a burglar. With my mask on.

No one laughed.

Because someone else was just like me.

You.

Not burned. But just sitting there with a mask around your face.

Where did you get it? I don't know. And you kept on wearing it for weeks.

And I have never said thank you. And tomorrow my parents are moving to England. I want you to know that I . . . No, scrub that.

You will get this when they dig up the time capsule. I want you to know that I . . . No, I just can't get it out.

Yours sincerely . . . No, scrub that.

Yours with thanks . . . No, scrub that.

Aw, what the heck . . .

Love,

Ben.

Well, that's what I wrote all those years ago. Something like that anyway. And here I am exactly nine years later. In the shopping centre. The school has gone. There is no Mr Wheeler and his grown-up class here to open the time capsule.

There is just me and a million shoppers. I can't even tell where the school was. It would take half an hour to walk from one end of the centre to another.

My face healed up long ago. I don't even have any scars. I should feel happy but the school has been knocked down. And there is no time capsule with my letter in it. I guess the bulldozers must have uncovered it. Or it could still be buried, deep under the shops and fountains and car parks. Maybe some of the letters inside were sent to the kids. Who knows? No one would have been able to contact me – on the other side of the world.

One of the other kids might be here in the shopping centre. Maybe, like me, they have come because they didn't know the school was knocked down. But I would never recognise them. Not after all these years. Not now we are grown.

I make my way sadly through the happy shoppers. I don't notice the shouting and jostling and laughing. I reach the door.

And for a moment my heart misses a beat.

For standing there I see something that takes me back in time. Silently standing by the door is a person wearing a burns bandage on her face. Children are staring at her. They shouldn't do that. Neither should I. But my heart is beating fast and I don't know what I am doing.

80

The woman's eyes meet mine and slowly she starts to take off the bandage. The children gasp. And so do I as her hair falls down behind her like the golden tail of an angel's horse.

Just for a moment I am twelve again. I catch my breath. My stomach wobbles.

I stare at the woman in front of me.

I know that my life is going to be happy. Because she is smiling the biggest smile.

Just like me.

RINGING WET

1

The man next door buried his wife in the backyard.

That's what I reckon, anyway. Dad says I have a vivid imagination. And my rotten, horrible, worst-ever big brother says I am nuts.

But I am not nuts. No way. See, it starts like this. I am reading a book where five kids go on a holiday. They discover smugglers in some underground caves but the adults won't believe them. Everyone thinks they are crazy. But in the end they catch the smugglers and become heroes. All the parents and police have to say sorry.

Since I read that book I have been on the lookout. To be honest there are not many smugglers around our way. I have looked and looked. There are not even any underground tunnels.

But there is Mr Grunge next door. He moved in two months ago. He acts in a very suspicious way. Consider these facts:

1. Mr Grunge has a crabby face.
2. He never comes out in the daytime.
3. He shouts at his wife in a loud, horrible voice.
4. His wife does all of the shopping and washing-up and cooking.
5. Mr Grunge just sits there all day watching TV.
6. Two days ago Mrs Grunge disappears.
   Yes, DISAPPEARS.
7. The night that his wife disappears Mr Grunge digs in the backyard.
   Yes, DIGS IN THE GARDEN *AT NIGHT*.

I know all this because I have been spying on them through a chink in their curtains.

Yes, it all fits in. They have an argument. He hits her with the frying-pan or something. Then he drags her out into the backyard. He takes off her diamond bracelet and buries her. I do not actually see this happen. But I put two and two together. It is the only explanation.

'Don't be crazy, Misty,' says Dad. 'She's probably gone on a holiday.'

'In the middle of winter?' I say.

'She could have gone to Queensland to get a bit of sun,' says Dad.

'Without her best diamond bracelet?' I say.

Dad looks at me through narrow eyes. 'How do you know she hasn't taken her bracelet?' he says.

'She's been peeping through the window,' says Simon, my rotten worst-ever brother.

Dad bangs down his paper on the table. He is as mad as a hatter. 'Misty,' he yells. 'That is a terrible thing to do. Spying and going into someone else's garden.'

Simon is such a dobber. He always spoils things. He is a real wet blanket. I decide to pay him back. 'Well, *he* got a detention at school yesterday,' I yell. 'For not doing his homework.'

Dad is really mad now. He rolls his eyes. 'What a way to start the school holidays,' he roars. 'Go to your rooms at once. Both of you.'

I stomp off to my bedroom and almost slam the door. There is an exact amount of noise you can make when you are almost slamming the door. If you do it too loud your parents will stop your pocket money for a month. If you get it right they cannot be quite sure that you actually slammed the door and they won't do anything. But it still annoys them.

My Dad is so stubborn. So is Simon. They won't believe that Mr Grunge has buried his wife in the garden. There is only one thing for me to do. One night, when there is no moon. When it is very dark. I will go and dig her up. Yes, DIG HER UP.

2

I am lying there in bed thinking about how I will dig up the body when Simon bursts into the room. He has his fingers held out like claws. 'Ticky, ticky, ticky,' he says with a nasty look on his face.

'No, Simon. No, no, no,' I scream. 'Not that. Don't. Please, please. I'm sorry I dobbed.'

'Ticky, ticky, ticky,' says Simon. Oh, he is so awful. He is bigger than me. Almost as big as Dad. I just can't stand up to him. I curl up in a ball on the bed. It is my only defence.

Simon gets his horrible fingers in under my armpits and starts to tickle. I hate it. I just hate it. I start to scream and kick and yell. 'Don't,' I yell. 'You pain. Dad, Dad, Dad.' I stop yelling. I am laughing. I don't want to laugh. I want to scream. But his fingers are digging in and I just can't help it.

I squirm and kick. And then I do it. I knew I would do it. And so did Simon. It is why he is tickling me. I always do it when someone tickles me.

I wet my pants. Yes, WET MY PANTS. Warm wet wee runs down my legs and onto the bed. Oh, it is terrible.

Simon sees. 'What's that?' he mocks. 'Where did that come from?' He laughs wickedly and then runs out the door.

I throw a pillow after him. 'You wait,' I say. 'You just wait.'

I hang my head in my hands. I am so ashamed. I always wet myself when someone tickles me. Even if I just get excited I do it. The doctor says I will grow out of it. Probably I will. By the time I am fifty.

There is something else, too. Even worse. Every night I wet the bed. It is awful. Just awful. In the mornings I wake up and everything is wet. I hate it.

I hate it. I hate it. I hate it.

Last year I couldn't go on the school camp. I was just too embarrassed.

I have a shower and change my clothes. Then I go into the lounge to see Dad. 'Something has to be done,' I say. 'Can't you do something to stop this bed-wetting? It is ruining my life.'

Dad nods his head. 'There is one more thing to try,' he says. 'I have been hoping we wouldn't need it. But I guess we have to give it a go.'

'Anything,' I say. 'I will try anything.'

3

That night Dad comes home with a rubber blanket. 'We put this under your sheet,' says Dad. 'When you wee it makes the blanket wet and it will ring a bell. You wake up and we change the sheets. After a couple of weeks your brain knows what is going to happen and it stops you wetting. Bingo – you are cured.'

I don't like the sound of it. Not one bit. But I am desperate. I will try anything. I snuggle down under the covers. Outside the moon is shining bright. It is not dark enough to go and dig in the neighbour's garden. So I close my eyes and drop off to sleep.

'Ding, ding, ding, ding.' Good grief. What is it? That terrible noise. I sit bolt upright in bed. It is like sirens from the police, the ambulance and the fire brigade all put together. My head is spinning. Is the house on fire or what?

I know. I know. I bet the police have come to arrest Mr Grunge. They will charge him with murder.

Dad bursts into the room with a smile. 'It works,' he says. 'Out you hop, sweetheart. You go and change your pyjamas and I'll put on fresh sheets.'

My heart sinks. It is not the police. I have wet the bed. The terrible noise comes from the bell attached to the rubber blanket. It works all right. It is the worst noise in the world.

Dad makes the bed while I put on dry pyjamas. 'See, that wasn't so bad,' says Dad as he walks out. He is quite chirpy really.

I snuggle down under the clean, crisp sheets. I am so tired. This getting up in the middle of the night takes it out of you. I have no sooner closed my eyes than 'ding, ding, ding, ding'. Oh no. I've wet the bed again. I look at the clock. Two hours. Have two hours really passed already?

Dad staggers into the room. This time he is not so chirpy. 'Geeze,' he says. 'I'd just dropped off to sleep. Okay, up you get. I'll get some dry sheets.' Dad is not exactly cross. Well, he is trying not to be cross. But I can tell that he does not like getting up in the middle of the night. And he is not the only one – that's for sure.

The next day is Saturday. It is Mum's weekend. Mum and Dad split up a couple of years ago and we live with Dad. Every second Saturday we go off with Mum. It is grouse because she takes us to lots of good places. To be honest, though, I wish she still lived at home.

Dad looks out of the window. 'Here's your mother,' he says. He never calls her Mum any more. He always calls her *your mother*. Funny that. Anyway, Simon and I race out and hop into Mum's car.

'Where are we going?' says Simon.

'Luna Park,' says Mum.

'Unreal,' we both yell.

We wander through the great big mouth that is the entrance to Luna Park and look around. We have a ride on the Big Dipper, the Water Caves and go into the Giggle Palace. They are all great.

'Let's go on the Rotor,' says Simon.

'What's that?' says Mum.

'It's this round room,' I say. 'You stick to the wall. I am not going on it. No way.'

'Neither am I,' says Mum.

'Wimps,' says Simon. 'I'm going on it. You can watch if you like. You can go upstairs and look down on the brave ones.' He bends one arm and bulges out his muscle. He thinks he is so tough.

4

We all get in the line, pay our money and file inside. The line splits into two. One line is for the people who are going to stick to the wall. The other is for those who want to watch. There is a lot of pushing and shoving and Mum is not sure where we are. 'You go in there,' says Simon.

Mum and I file through a door while Simon heads up some stairs. The door slams behind us. We look around. We are in a big, round room with about ten others. There are a whole lot of people up above looking down on us. It is sort of like a round squash court with spectators sitting around upstairs.

What is going on here? What has happened?

Simon has tricked us. That's what. I see his grinning face peering down from the spectators' seats. He thinks he is so smart. He has sent us into the wrong place. We are inside the Rotor. Yes, INSIDE.

I start to panic. I have to get out of here. I just have to. But where is the door? I can't even see it. There is no handle. And the walls are covered in rubber.

A loud voice comes over the microphone. 'All riders stand against the wall, please,' it says. Riders? I am not meant to be a rider. I am meant to be a watcher. 'Let me out,' I yell.

But it is too late. Mum drags me back to the wall and the room starts to spin. Faster and faster. The faces up above are just a blur. We are whirling around like a crazy spinning top. Suddenly the floor drops away. And we are stuck to the wall. Right up in the air.

This is terrible. Horrible. I am scared. I'm embarrassed. Everyone is looking at us. We are like flies on the wall.

Mum starts to squirm. She has turned sideways. If she is not careful she will soon be upside down. Some of the people on the wall are groaning. Others are screaming. Some are laughing and having fun.

But I am not having fun. I am excited. When I am excited something terrible always happens.

And it does happen. Oh, horror of horrors. It happens. I wet my pants.

There on the wall with everyone looking – I wet my pants.

A river of warm wet wee runs along the wall. It snakes its way towards Mum. My shame scribbles its hateful way across the round, spinning room.

I close my eyes and try to pretend that this is not happening. But it is.

After ages and ages the walls start to slow. Gradually the floor comes up to meet us. Finally the Rotor stops and I am standing on the floor in front of a wet, smeared wall. My legs and dress are all wet. Mum and I stagger outside and blink in the sunlight.

Simon is going to die. Simon is history. I will get him for this.

Before I can reach Simon to strangle him, Mum grabs him by the shoulders and shakes him until his head just about drops off. 'You have ruined the day,' she yells. 'Now I will have to take you back to your father's so that Misty can change.'

We all drive home without talking. I am so angry. 'I will get you for this, Simon,' I think to myself. 'I will get you for this. If it is the last thing I do, I will pay you back.'

5

Mum drops us at the gate and drives off. As we walk up the drive I see Dad's startled face staring out of the window. I also see Mr Grunge in his backyard. He has a shovel in his hand. He stares at me as I go by. It is almost like he can read my mind. I shiver and hurry indoors.

Dad is surprised to see us. 'What are you doing back so soon?' he says. He is annoyed. And I know why. In the lounge-room is his girlfriend, Brook. She only ever comes over when we are out. Her hair is all ruffled and she looks embarrassed. Dad's shirt is hanging out. They have been cuddling. Yes, CUDDLING. And we have broken it up.

I am annoyed too. He should be pleased to see us back. Not annoyed.

'Simon made me wet my pants,' I yell.

'I did not,' he says.

'Liar, liar, liar,' I shout.

Dad rolls his eyeballs at Brook. Then he does something strange. He takes out his wallet. He bangs a fifty-dollar note down on the table. 'See this?' he says. 'This is for the person who keeps quiet the longest.'

Simon and I stop yelling. We are both very interested.

'The first one to speak,' says Dad, 'does not get the fifty-dollar note. As soon as one of you speaks, the other one gets this. Do you understand?'

I open my mouth to say 'yes'. But I don't. No way. I just nod my head in silence. So does Simon.

'Not one word,' says Dad. 'Not a shout, not a scream, not a giggle. Total silence. That is the deal. Get it?'

We both nod our heads again.

Dad looks smug. 'Now maybe we will get some peace at last,' he says.

I grin an evil grin. Now I will get Simon back. I will win the fifty dollars and he will be really cut. It is perfect. He might be bigger than me. He might be stronger. He might even be smarter. But I am stubborn. I will not say a word to anyone. Even if it takes ten years.

That night I get into bed and wriggle down under the blankets. I turn off the lights and my mind starts to wander. Mr Grunge was giving me a funny look this afternoon. What was he thinking about? Suddenly I feel cold all over.

He knows.

He knows that I know that he has buried his wife in the backyard.

91

What if I am next?

I can't sleep. I toss and turn. Finally I drift off when ...
'crash'. My bedroom door flies open. Someone bursts
into the room. My brain freezes with fear. It is a person
wearing a devil's mask. A horrible, horrible mask. The
figure dances around at the end of my bed.

Suddenly I am not scared any more. I have seen that
mask before. Simon bought it at the Show. He is trying
to make me scream. He wants me to yell out. So that he
can get the money. But it won't work. I turn on the light
and take out a pencil and paper. 'Buzz off, Simon,' I write
in large letters.

Simon pulls off the mask and pulls a face at me. Then
he leaves.

6

It takes me ages and ages but finally I fall off to sleep.

'Ding, ding, ding, ding.' What, what, what? Rats. It is
the bed-wetting alarm again. Already. What a racket. It's
enough to wake the dead.

Dad comes in and turns on the light. He holds a finger
up to his lips. 'Don't say a word,' he says. 'Remember the
fifty dollars.' He sure is taking this seriously.

I put on a clean pair of pyjamas and Dad changes the
sheets. Then he goes off to bed. Brook must have gone
home.

An hour ticks by. And then another. I just can't get off
to sleep. Too much has happened. I have wet my pants
on the Rotor. Dad was cross because we came home early.

Simon is a horrible worst-ever brother. Mr Grunge knows that I am on to him. My life is a total mess.

If only I was rich or beautiful or famous.

Outside it is dark. There is no moon.

Famous.

That's it. Tonight is the night. I will sneak out into Mr Grunge's garden. I will dig up his wife before he can come and get me. I will be famous. I bet there will be a reward. And it will be worth at least fifty dollars. Maybe more.

I get dressed, push up the window and sneak out into the night. Down to the shed for a shovel. Up over the fence. This is easy. It is dark. Very dark.

The garden is as silent as a graveyard. A little shiver runs up my spine. This is not easy. This is scary. Where is the grave? Where is the spot where Mr Grunge has buried Mrs Grunge? Where is Mr Grunge?

I feel my way around. Gradually my eyes grow used to the dark. There it is. Over there. Crafty. What a crafty devil. He has planted tomato plants on top of the grave. And tied them up to stakes. He is trying to make everyone think it is just a vegetable garden. But he can't fool me. I know it is a grave.

Graves are spooky things. Maybe this is not such a good idea. What if Mr Grunge is nearby? Watching. Waiting. I peep over my shoulder. What was that? Nothing. Terrible thoughts enter my mind. If Mr Grunge catches me I will be history. What will he plant on *my* grave?

Run, run, run for it. No, stay. You will never sleep at night until this mystery is solved. I lean over the vegetable garden. I take a deep breath and rip out the little seedlings and the stakes. Then I start to dig.

It is slow, hard work. As I dig I start to think. What will I find? What if I suddenly uncover a horrible white hand? What if I hit a nose? What if there are staring, dead eyes down there? With dirt in them.

I dig more and more slowly. I don't want to find Mrs Grunge. But I do, too. I am so scared. There is a rustle in the bushes. What was that?

'Aargh,' I scream. Eyes. Someone's eyes. Staring at me from the bushes.

I drop my shovel and run. I scream and scream and scream. I am up and over that fence before you can blink. I am through that window and back into bed before you can snap your fingers.

I have my eyes closed. I want to fall asleep. And quickly. There is going to be big trouble. I can feel it in my bones.

7

There is a knock on the front door. I hear footsteps. I hear the front door open. I hear voices. Oh no. This is terrible. I have had it.

Footsteps approach my bedroom. Someone comes into the room and turns on the light. I pretend to be asleep but through my closed eyelashes I see Dad. He is carrying a shovel. He is looking at the open window. 'I know you're awake, Misty,' he says. 'Come with me.'

Dad pulls me out of bed towards the lounge-room. 'Mr Grunge is here,' he says. 'Someone has gone and ruined his tomato patch. A vandal has dug it up.'

I pull my hand away from Dad and tear back to the

bedroom. I grab a bit of paper and a pencil. 'He murdered his wife,' I write. 'I was digging her up.'

Dad reads the note and throws it onto the floor. Then he drags me into the lounge. 'This is Mr Grunge,' says Dad. Mr Grunge is sitting there on the sofa. He is not saying anything. He is staring at me with evil eyes. Why can't Dad see it? Anyone would know that Mr Grunge was a murderer just by looking at him.

I open my mouth to speak. I open my mouth to tell Dad to call the police. That will prove it once and for all. They can dig up the vegetable patch.

But I do not get a chance to say anything. Dad goes on and on and on. Talk about trouble. Boy, do I cop it. I am a vandal. I am hopeless. I am mean. I am ungrateful. I will have to plant out a new garden. Just when Dad is starting to get some happiness in his life, I ruin everything. It seems like the lecture will never end. I start to cry. Silent tears run down my cheeks. In the end Dad feels sorry for me and sends me off to bed.

I hear Dad and Mr Grunge talking in the lounge. The front door slams. I look out of the window and see Mr Grunge walking down the front path. 'Murderer,' I think to myself. I just know that Mrs Grunge is dead and buried in the vegetable patch.

But no one will believe me.

Why doesn't anything nice ever happen to me? Why does everything have to go wrong?

There is only one good thing about the whole episode.

I didn't say a word. I didn't even cry out loud. I am still in the running for the fifty dollars. I will get that fifty dollars and pay Simon back if it kills me.

Once again I try to fall off to sleep. More hours tick by but sleep won't come. My mind is too full of misery.

Suddenly I hear something. A rustle outside. There is someone in the garden.

And my window is still open. Yes, MY WINDOW IS STILL OPEN.

The skin seems to crawl over my bones. I am shivering with fear. What is outside? Who is outside?

It is him. I just know it is him. It is Mr Grunge. My throat is dry. I am petrified with fear. He is coming. He is coming. He is coming.

A dark figure appears at the window. A figure wearing a balaclava. The intruder puts a leg through the window. I open my mouth to scream out, 'Dad, Dad, Dad.'

But I don't call out. I don't say a word.

My heart is beating like a million hammers. I am so scared. But I am not stupid. My mind is working over-time. Because of the balaclava I don't really know who it is. This could be Simon again. It could be him trying to make me call out for Dad. So that he can get the fifty dollars.

Oh, what will I do? If it is Mr Grunge I will end up in the vegetable patch. But if it is Simon I will lose the bet when I call out. And he will get the money.

What will I do? What, what what?

I know. Suddenly it comes to me. I know what to do.

And I do it. Yes, I do it.

ON PURPOSE.

I wet my pants. Wonderful warm wee runs down between my legs.

'Ding, ding, ding, ding.' What a racket. It is like sirens

from the police, the ambulance and the fire brigade all put together.

The intruder straightens up with a jerk, bangs into the window and slumps to the ground – out like a light.

Dad bursts into the room. 'What in the . . . ?' he says. Then he sees the figure on the floor. We stare down. Who is under that balaclava? Is it Simon? Or is it Mr Grunge? Is it a man or is it a boy?

Dad bends down and pulls up the balaclava. We both stare with wide open eyes. It is not a man. And it is not a boy.

Just then Simon bursts into the room and looks at the burglar.

'Mrs Grunge,' he yells.

Yes, *MRS* GRUNGE. She is not dead. She is not buried. She is out like a light on the floor. Her diamond bracelet glints in the moonlight.

I am still sitting up in my wet bed. Okay, I was wrong. Mrs Grunge is not buried in the garden. She is not dead. I made a mistake. But I grin. Something good has happened.

'You spoke first,' I say to my rotten worst-ever, wet-blanket brother.

Simon looks as if his face is going to fall off. He is so cut.

Well, after that everything is fantastic. The police come and arrest Mr and Mrs Grunge. Then they dig up their backyard. They find lots of jewellery and watches and video recorders. 'We have been looking for these thieves for a long time,' says the police chief. 'There is a big reward. Two thousand dollars.'

Yes, TWO THOUSAND.

So I get the reward. And the fifty dollars as well. And my picture is in the paper and I am on television. Dad and Brook and Mum are so proud of me.

And just to top it all off, I never wet the bed again.

Yes, NEVER.

BACKWARD STEP

If you went back in time and stopped your
grandparents from meeting each other you
would never have been born.
But then if you had never been born you wouldn't
be able to go back and stop them.
Would you?

'John,' said Mrs Booth to her five-year-old son. 'You just
sit there and watch "Inspector Gadget" on the TV while I
go down the street and get some milk. I'll be back by the
time it's over.'

'I love "Inspector Gadget",' said John.

Mrs Booth reached the front gate and then stopped. She
felt a little guilty, leaving her son alone in the house. But
she knew he wouldn't budge. Not for another twenty
minutes. Not until the show was over.

'Excuse me, Mrs Booth,' said a voice.

She jumped in fright and then stared into the eyes of a teenage boy. He thrust an old exercise book into her hand. 'Read this. Please, please, please read it.'

'I'm not interested in buying . . . ' she began to say.

'I'm not selling anything,' he said. 'And it's not a religion. This is important. This can save your life. You're in great danger. Please read it.'

'Now?' she said.

'Right away. Please, it's really important.'

There was something about the boy. He seemed very nervous. And she felt as if she knew him. The boy's hands were shaking. 'Well,' she said. 'Just for a second.' She gave a little sigh and opened the old exercise book.

1

I am fourteen. Nine years ago I was also fourteen. And nine years before that I was fourteen too.

It is creepy. It is weird. But I think I have figured it all out. It makes sense to me now. It is the only explanation. No one will believe me, of course. They will just say I am crazy.

Look – I'll try and explain it to you as simply as I can. I've put one and one together and come up with two. Or should I say I've put nine and five together and come up with five.

No, no, no, that's just talking in riddles. I'll start at the beginning. Or is it the end?

Sorry, there I go again. Look, have you ever wanted strange powers? You know, to be able to fly or read thoughts or be very strong? I'll bet you think it would be great. But think again. It could be dangerous. You could end up hurting yourself. Like I did.

I am famous. Yes, there wouldn't be too many people around here who haven't heard of me. I'll bet you think it would be great to be famous. Pictures in the paper. On television. People wanting your autograph. That sort of thing.

It's not really that good. You never know whether people want to be your friend because they like you or because you are well known. And then there are kids who get jealous and give you a hard time and push you around. I would rather be ordinary and have ordinary problems.

I became famous at five. They called me the boy from nowhere. There was a great fuss. It was in the papers. A five-year-old boy just suddenly appeared sitting in the back seat of the class. Right next to a girl called Sharon Coppersmith.

That boy was me.

Sharon Coppersmith screamed and screamed when I arrived. Or appeared. According to her I just popped out of nowhere. One minute the seat was empty. The next minute there was little old me. Five years old, sitting next to her in a history class.

All the big kids crowded around. They were glad to have something break up the lesson. They laughed and offered me lollies and made a great fuss. The teacher thought that I had wandered in from the street.

I just looked up and started crying. I was only five but I remember it just like it was yesterday. Who were all these big kids? Where was my Mummy? Where was the nice big boy who wanted to help me?

'What's your name, little fella?' said the teacher.

For a while I couldn't get a word out. I just sat there sobbing. In the end I managed to say, 'John Boof, Firteen Tower Street, Upwey, seven five four, oh, oh, six two free free.'

'John Booth,' said the teacher. '13 Tower Street Upwey. Phone 754 006233. Well done. Don't cry, little fella. We'll have you home in no time.'

2

The principal's office seemed huge. He wore a pair of those little half-moon glasses and kept peeping over them at me while he spoke into the phone. 'Are you sure?' he said. '754 006233. No John Booth? Never heard of him. How long have you lived there? Three years. Well, sorry to have troubled you.'

I just kept licking the salty tears that were rolling down my cheek and wondering how I got there.

I had been watching 'Inspector Gadget' on television. I remember the man saying something like, 'a brand new episode'. Then a big boy was talking to me. He just popped out of nowhere. He was nice. I was holding his hand and then 'poof', he was gone and there I was sitting in this school-room full of big kids. With everyone looking at me and wondering where I had come from.

'Look,' said the principal to his secretary. 'Pop him in your car and see if he can show you where he lives. If he can't find the place you'll have to take him to the police station. His parents will come for him sooner or later.'

I knew that I didn't have a father. But I didn't know that my mother had died nine years earlier.

The secretary was nice. She strapped me into the seat next to her and gave me a little white bag with jelly-beans in it. 'Don't worry, love,' she said. 'We'll soon find Mum. You just show me the way to go. All you have to do is point.'

She drove around for a bit and I thought I recognised some of the houses and places. But they were different. Looking back I can describe it as like being in a dream. The streets were the same but different.

'There,' I suddenly yelled. It was the water tower. I could see it in the distance. It was right next to our house.

'What?' said the nice lady. 'The water tower? You couldn't live there, love.'

'Neks door,' I said.

She smiled. 'Now we're getting somewhere.'

There was only one house next to the water tower and it was my house. At least it was like my house. It had the same rock chimney and the same fountain in the front yard. But it was painted green instead of blue. And the trees were huge. And the chicken shed had gone. But it was still my house.

'Mummy,' I shouted. I had never been so happy in my life. I didn't stop to think that you can't paint a house in one day. And that trees can't grow overnight. When you are five you think adults can do anything. I pelted up to the front door and ran inside. Then I just stopped and stared. Our furniture had gone. There was no television. My photo wasn't on the wall.

'Mummy,' I screamed. 'Mummy, Mummy, Mummy.' I scampered into the kitchen. A very old lady looked down at me. Then she looked at the secretary who had followed me in and started to scream.

The old lady thought we had come to rob her.

After all, we had just walked into her house without even knocking.

3

Well, after a lot of talking, the secretary managed to calm the old lady down. They had a cup of tea and the old lady gave me some green cordial. 'Mummy,' I said. 'I want my mummy.' I didn't know what this old lady was doing in our house. I didn't know where my toys had gone. I didn't like the new carpet and the photos of strange people. I wanted everything to be like it was before. I also wanted to go to the toilet.

I ran upstairs, through the big bedroom and into the little toilet at the back. When I came back I heard the secretary saying, 'How did he know where to go?'

The old lady just shook her head. None of us knew what was going on.

The secretary took me out to the car but I didn't want to get in. I didn't want to leave the house that was supposed to be my home. But the secretary was firm and she put me in the front seat. As we drove off she checked the house number. '13 Tower Street,' she said to herself with a puzzled look.

The police were puzzled too. 'We'll look him up on our computer,' said the sergeant. 'His parents have probably reported him missing by now.'

He tapped away for several minutes. Then he scratched his head and just sat there staring at the screen. 'There is a John Booth missing,' he said. 'He disappeared nine years ago, aged five. That would make him fourteen by now.'

'Well, this little boy is not fourteen,' said the secretary. She squatted down and looked into my eyes. 'Are you, John?'

'I'm five,' I said.

The sergeant tapped for a while longer. 'The missing boy lived around here,' he said. '13 Tower Street.' He crouched down and patted me on the head. 'Where were you when you lost your mum?' he asked kindly.

'Watching "Inspector Gadget",' I said.

'Is that still on?' said the secretary.

The sergeant rummaged through a newspaper. 'No channel has "Inspector Gadget" on,' he said. 'Not any time this week.'

'Maybe he's from another state,' said the secretary.

The sergeant went off for a while and the secretary tried to read me a story. But I didn't want it. I only wanted my mother. Finally the sergeant returned. 'I rang Channel Two,' he said. ' "Inspector Gadget" is showing in fifteen countries but nowhere in Australia. The nearest place is New Zealand.'

'Maybe he's a Kiwi,' said the secretary.

The sergeant squatted down again. 'Say fish and chips,' he said.

'Fish and chips,' I said.

'Nah,' said the sergeant. 'He's a dinkie di Aussie, aren't you, mate?'

I didn't know what it meant but I nodded anyway.

After that the secretary left and a policewoman looked after me. Everyone was getting more and more excited. 'Wait until the papers get a hold of this,' said the sergeant.

They were looking at an old newspaper. There was a picture of a mangled car. And a picture of five-year-old me standing in front of the water tower.

The sergeant shook his head. 'A kid goes missing nine years ago,' he said. 'Then an identical kid turns up today. He says he lives at the same address. He says he has the same name. He knows all about "Inspector Gadget" which hasn't been shown here for nine years. He is even wearing the same clothes. This boy is the world's first time traveller. He has jumped forward nine years.'

There was one thing they didn't tell me for a long time. I wanted my mum but they couldn't go and fetch her. She was killed the day I disappeared. A car knocked her down while she was crossing the road to the milk bar.

Talk about a fuss. Everyone wanted to see me. Take my photo. People from the university wanted to study me. Fortune tellers and mystics claimed they had moved me in time. I was on television all over the world.

In the end my grandma came and got me. At first I didn't recognise her because she was much greyer and had more wrinkles. But as soon as she spoke I knew it was her. 'You're coming with me, John Boy,' she said. There was no arguing with that voice. I ran over and hugged and hugged her until my arms ached.

She tried to stop them taking photos. She tried to keep off the professors and psychics. She tried to give me a normal life. But of course she couldn't. She was old and she didn't really want to bring up a child again. 'Your mother was enough,' she said. 'Having a child and looking after it with no father. And now it's me looking after you.'

So here I am nine years later. An oddity. Grandma is doing her best. But she is old and tired and we are both unhappy. I have no friends. No mother. No father. I'm famous. Everybody knows me. But nobody likes me. Being famous has mucked up my life.

Nine years ago I travelled in time. Today I found out that I can do it again.

4

I was walking along the street in a sort of a daze. There was a lot of traffic. Trucks, cars, motorbikes. The air was full of fumes and noise. I checked the time on my watch. Four o'clock.

A huge petrol tanker was bearing down. I didn't see it. I just stepped out in front of it without looking. There was a squeal of brakes. Blue smoke and a blaring horn. There was no time to get out of the way.

I knew that I was gone. There was no escape.

Suddenly, 'poof'.

I was lying on a seat on the other side of the road. An old man sitting next to me looked as if a ghost had just appeared in front of him. He screamed and ran off as fast as he could go.

What had happened? How did I get there?

I looked at my watch. Half past four. Where had that half hour gone?

Suddenly it all fell into place. I was the boy who could travel in time. I must have been run over by the truck and badly injured. Maybe people had carried me over to the bench. I would have wished that I could go back in time to just before the moment I stepped in front of the truck. And that's what happened. For just a second there would have been two of me on the footpath. The injured me would have grabbed the hand of the other me before he was hit. And wished ourselves half an hour in the future.

But then the injured me would never have been injured. In fact he would have missed those thirty minutes too. So he never did any of it. He never happened. He must have disappeared as soon as I landed on the seat where he had started from.

And the old man saw a boy appearing out of nowhere. I had come from half an hour in the past.

I had gone back in time. And saved myself by bringing me into the future. I could travel in time just by wishing it to happen. There was no doubt about it. Thirty minutes. If I could do thirty minutes I could do eighteen years. I could go back to the time when I was watching 'Inspector Gadget'. I could stop my mother going to the shop. Then she wouldn't be killed and I wouldn't have to live with Grandma. I would be happy growing up with my mother.

But what if it went wrong? What if I made a mistake and arrived too late? Something deep inside was warning me. I felt as if I had been in this situation before. I was cautious. Then it struck me.

I *had* been there before.

I remember me at age five watching 'Inspector Gadget'. It was just as the closing credits were rolling. The end of the show. A big boy had just appeared out of nowhere. He was upset. He was searching around the house calling out 'Mum'. He looked out of the window. There was a policeman coming up the drive.

Suddenly I realised what had happened all those years ago. The fourteen-year-old me had gone back nine years in time. But I had arrived too late. 'Inspector Gadget' was over. My mother was dead. A policeman was coming up the drive to tell the five-year-old me that his mother was dead. I wouldn't have let that happen. I wouldn't have left him to live all those years with an old grandma who didn't want him. That's when I would have panicked. When I didn't think clearly.

I must have grabbed my hand. The big me must have grabbed the hand of the little me. And wished us nine years into the future. I wanted to take the five-year-old into the future and look after him.

'Poof.' The five-year-old me landed nine years into the future. The fourteen-year-old me just vanished. By taking his five-year-old self nine years into the future he ceased to exist. He had missed all those nine years and hadn't grown up. He was the boy who never was.

Suddenly a five-year-old child landed in the future. On his own. He didn't know how he got there. And neither did anyone else.

That's what I think happened anyway. That's my explanation of how I jumped nine years.

5

I went home and sat in my room. Grandma was taking a rest. She was tired. Much too tired to be worried about me.

What if I went back again? What if I was really careful? What if I went back to the front gate just as my mother reached it? At the beginning of 'Inspector Gadget'. I could tell her not to go to the milk bar. Then she would not be run over.

I closed my eyes and wished myself back.

Mrs Booth closed the exercise book and stood up. She could hear the strident voices of 'Inspector Gadget' floating through the window. She looked at the fourteen-year-old boy carefully. She was sure that she had seen him before. But she was a little cross. 'Why have you picked on our family?' she said. 'You have described me and my mother and my child. You've been snooping around. Why didn't you do your assignment on your own family?'

The fourteen-year-old boy was crying. 'You are my own family, Mum,' he said.

She still gripped the exercise book tightly in her hand. Her mind was in a spin. The boy was crying real tears.

'Your story doesn't make sense,' she said. 'If I go back inside, obviously I won't get run over. And none of what you have written will happen.'

'That's right,' he said.

'And you will never have been here.'

The boys lips trembled just a little. 'That's what I want,' he said.

Mrs Booth turned and walked back to the house. When she reached the door she turned and looked back. She felt as if she had been talking to someone.

But there was no one there.

PUBIC HARE

Why couldn't I be called Peter Smith or Peter Jones? Or even Peter Rabbit? Why did it have to be Peter Hare? Why oh why oh why?

1

'Okay, boys,' says the Phys. Ed. teacher. 'Take off all your clothes and hang them on your peg. Then make your way to the showers.'

What? With nothing on? On the first day at a new school? In front of everyone? Waltz across the changing room in the nude? Just like walking down the street as if everything is normal? I can't do it. I just can't.

The other boys all start to undress. They don't seem to care about being in the nuddy. They just drop their pants and hang them up without a thought. Some of them have started to head towards the showers already.

'Right, boys,' says the Phys. Ed. teacher. 'There are five showers. All line up in front of the first one. When I blow the whistle you move to the next shower. Each shower is a little cooler than the one before it. The last shower has no hot water at all. That will freshen you up a bit.'

The kids all start to moan and groan. 'Torture,' says Simons, the first boy in line.

'No wimps here,' says the Phys. Ed. teacher. 'And hurry up, all you stragglers.'

The line waiting for the showers grows longer and longer. Nearly all the boys are standing there, as naked as the day they were born. But I can't do it. I just can't. I take off one shoe, slowly. Then I pull off the other. Now I am the only boy still dressed. The others are all lined up, laughing and joking. In the raw.

The Phys. Ed. teacher looks at me. 'Come on, Hare. Hurry up. What are you waiting for?' he says.

Everyone looks at me. Every single boy. I can feel my face burning.

'No need to be embarrassed,' says the Phys. Ed. teacher. 'We're all the same. No one has anything that the others don't.'

If only this was true. But it isn't. I am different to all of them. Slowly I take off my clothes. I am standing there in my jocks. All alone. I lower my underpants and try to hide my nakedness with my hand. But it doesn't work. Everyone can see my shame.

Not one other boy is like me. I am the only one with hair. No one else has it. Not where I do. I am not talking about hair on the head. We all have that. But hair in other places – if you know what I mean.

I hold my hands over my private parts. A couple of boys are sniggering. They have seen. Oh, the shame of it. 'Pubic Hare,' says Simons. Everyone laughs. Even the teacher thinks it is funny although he tries to cover it up. Why did I have to be called Peter Hare?

'Check out the legs,' says someone else.

I have skinny, hairy legs. I have skinny arms. I have ribs that stick out. I am a total wreck. I am a physical wimp. An embarrassed bag of bones. The Phys. Ed. teacher blows the whistle and we all move forward.

How I wish I was hairless. And big and handsome. Like Simons and all the others. But I am just a little wimp. I am all alone. And the only boy in Year Seven with pubic hair. My face is so red you could warm your hands on it.

2

When I arrive home Mum gives me her usual lecture. 'Why don't you go out and play with the other children, dear?'

I give a smile. 'I have to go and concentrate,' I say.

'Concentrate,' she shouts. 'You just sit in your room staring at the wall. You will never get friends like that. Go out and play,' she says.

'Kids my age don't play,' I say.

'What do they do then?' she asks.

I think for a bit. 'Muck around,' I say.

Mum gets really cross at this point. 'Well, for heaven's sake go out and muck around.'

Mum will never understand. The other kids will just mock someone with pubic hair. Especially Simons. He will just give me heaps if I show my face. Or anything else for that matter. I head off to my room to stare at the wall.

Actually, staring at the wall is what I do best. But I also stare at other things. I have been staring at a leaf, a pin and a pen. Nothing has happened yet but I am sure it will. See, my idea is this. I reckon that it is possible to make things move by willpower. If you concentrate hard enough.

A wise man called Riah Devahs is teaching me this skill. He says that anyone can move things with their mind if they try hard enough. You just stare at something and think about it moving.

Riah Devahs can't actually show me how to do it. 'Everyone has to find their own path,' he says. He can do it himself. But he is not allowed to actually show me how.

'Mind over matter', it is called. You can do all sorts of things just by concentrating. Riah Devahs says that you should start with simple things. Like making a bit of hair float up into the air. Or moving pins. Then you can move on to bigger and better projects. I know that everyone will admire me if I can move things with my mind. Once I can do it I will be popular. You bet.

I stare at a pin on my desk. Then I start to think. 'Move pin. Move pin. Move pin.' That is all I am allowed to have in my mind. If any other thoughts creep into my brain then it won't work. 'Move pin. Move pin. Move pin. I wish I could stick this pin into Simons' bare backside. That would teach him to laugh at me for having pubic hair.' Oh no. I am thinking about Simons. I have let another thought creep in. I have to concentrate. Don't let other thoughts creep in.

I start again. 'Move pin. Move pin. Move pin.' My brain is just about busting. I have never concentrated so hard in my life. Not even the time when I subtracted four hundred and sixty-seven point five from seven hundred and two point one without even writing it down. Rats. I have done it again. I have stopped concentrating on the pin. I am thinking about sums. This will never work.

I will give it one more go. I close my eyes and screw up my eyelids. 'Move pin. Move pin. Move pin.'

I open my eyes and look at the pin. Look *for* the pin I should say. It has gone. It is not on the desk any more. It is on the floor. Did I move it with my mind? Or did I brush it with my arm? I am not quite sure. Nah, it was just my imagination.

Nothing is going right for me. Basically I am hopeless. I go and stare in the mirror. Look at me. Just look at me. Freckles everywhere. What a face. There should be somewhere you can go to get a new one. I would go down there and trade mine in. They probably wouldn't give me much for the old one, though. I can just hear the man in the face shop. 'Not much demand for turned-up noses, pointy ears and the first signs of a moustache,' he would say. 'I'll give you ten cents for it.'

I undo my belt and look down inside my underpants. The hair is still there. Ugly pubic hair. There seems to be more there every time I look.

I am looking down my pants. And Mum is looking at

me. How embarrassing. 'What on earth are you doing?' she says with a funny look on her face.

'Just a bit of staring,' I say.

I stare into the mirror again to make things seem a bit more normal. 'I'm ugly,' I say as I look at my reflection.

'No you're not, dear,' says Mum. 'You look just like your father.'

'That's what I mean,' I mumble under my breath.

Dad is a great bloke, but let's face it – he's no oil painting.

Mum is slowly getting mad. 'If you're not going to go out and play you can come and do the washing-up,' she says.

3

I decide to go out for a walk. Mothers can be so sneaky sometimes.

I will go and see Riah Devahs. That's what I will do. I have been a bit busy lately. I haven't seen him for about six weeks. He will be thinking I have forgotten all about him. He is a great bloke, is Riah Devahs. He wears a long green robe. He has a bald head and fifteen earrings.

He never leaves his little hut in the forest. He just sits there on the dirt floor with his eyes closed and his legs crossed. 'Og,' he says to himself. 'Og. Og. Og.' Over and over, he says it in his mind. This is his mantra. His special word. It is how he makes things move. He just thinks about his special word and he can move mountains. That's what he says anyway.

I am not allowed to use his special word. Everyone has to have their own. One day I will get mine.

I walk on through the bush. There are probably birds singing but I don't hear anything. I wander along concentrating on something else. 'Pubic hair vanish. Pubic hair vanish.' I say it over and over and over. Then I stop for a check. I look inside my jeans but the hair has not disappeared. If anything there is more than before. What a life. Geeze, it is tough to be a person sometimes.

When I get my own mantra – my own special word – I will be able to move things. Riah Devahs says that he will give me a mantra one day. 'When the time is right.' For the time being I will have to make do with 'Pubic hair vanish'. Even though it doesn't work.

I hurry on through the bush. Maybe Riah Devahs will give me my mantra today. Maybe the time is right. Maybe I will get the word that will help me to move things with my mind. I grin. I feel very lucky all of a sudden.

Finally I reach the hut. But something is wrong. There is chanting coming from inside. There are a lot of voices. Riah Devahs is not alone. There has never been anyone else but him in the hut before. Except for me.

I tiptoe up to the open door and look inside. My eyes grow wide at what I see. There are five holy men sitting in a circle. They all wear green robes and fifteen earrings. They are all bald. They are staring at an urn in the middle of the circle and chanting in deep voices.

Riah Devahs is not there. But I remember what he taught me. I must not interrupt the chanting. I stand on my head in the doorway. This is to show that I come in peace.

118

The chanting goes on and on. No one looks at me standing there on my head. The blood starts to run to my brain. To be perfectly honest I am not very good at standing on my head. My ears start to throb. Then my nose. I feel as if all of my blood is inside my head. I am sure that my skull is going to explode at any minute.

I can't last any longer. Crash. I collapse in a heap on the dirt floor. No one looks up. The holy men just keep chanting.

'Sorry,' I say. Talk about embarrassing. All the blood is still in my head. My face is so red that you could warm your feet on it. The holy men go on chanting. Nothing can stop them.

Finally they are finished. Silence falls over the hut. I say nothing. I just sit and wait.

Suddenly they all speak together as if in one voice. 'Welcome, brother Hare,' they say.

'Greetings, brothers,' I answer politely. 'Where is Riah Devahs?'

'He has moved on,' says one of the holy men.

My heart sinks inside me. 'Is he coming back?' I ask.

They all shake their heads.

Oh no. Now I will never get my mantra. I will never achieve mind over matter. Riah Devahs will not be there to give me the word I need.

Suddenly I have a thought. Maybe he has left a message. Maybe he left a message with my own special word written on it.

'This is for you,' says one of the holy men. He hands me the urn from the centre of the circle. I know that this is a present from Riah Devahs because his name is written on the side of the urn.

He has not forgotten me. 'Is my mantra inside?' I say excitedly.

'Each foot must find its own path to wisdom,' says a different holy man.

This means that I must go. This means that I cannot say another word. Riah Devahs always finished our sessions with those words. Once those words are uttered I must leave at once. No arguments. I take the urn and walk outside. I walk for a bit without looking back. Then I turn around. The holy men are filing off into the forest. I wonder if I will ever see them again. Their bald heads shine in the sun.

After a bit I sit down and look at the urn. I am excited. I just know that Riah Devahs has written my mantra and placed it in the urn. With trembling hands I pull off the lid.

My heart falls. Dust. It is filled with dust. Maybe something is buried in it. I rummage around in the dust with my fingers. It gets all over me. 'Achoo.' It makes me sneeze but that is all. There is no mantra. No paper. No words at all.

I put the lid back on and try to get the dust off my hands. Why did Riah give me this urn of dust? Why didn't he give me my word?

I look at his name written on the side. *Riah Devahs.* An idea starts to form in my mind. This is a puzzle. Each foot must find its own path to wisdom. There is an answer. Yes. Yes, yes, yes. My mantra is here somewhere. If only I can find it.

Where is it? Where, where, where?

Suddenly it hits me. It is there. On the side of the urn. Right in front of my eyes. *Riah Devahs*. They are the magic words. What could be better? My mantra is the name of my wise and holy teacher. I have solved the puzzle that he set for me. Riah Devahs has not let me down.

I stare at an ant that is crawling towards me. I concentrate very hard. I will make the ant turn around. 'Riah Devahs. Riah Devahs,' I chant to myself. I am concentrating so hard that my eyeballs bulge out.

The ant turns around and crawls off the other way.

Coincidence. I mean, it probably didn't like the look of me. And I wouldn't blame it either. Still, I might as well try something else. But before I have time to think I feel a sneeze coming. The dust is getting up my nose. 'Ah, ah, ah, choo.' Rats, I hate sneezing. So does Mum.

Mum. That reminds me. She said to be home by five-thirty. It is already five-forty. I clutch the urn to my chest and rush off as fast as I can go. It is best not to be too late. Especially when Mum is in a bad mood.

4

On the way home I pass the cemetery. There is a late evening funeral going on. The priest is reading from a book as the coffin lowers into the ground. 'Ashes to ashes. Dust to dust,' he says.

For some reason his words stick in my mind. They make me feel a bit uncomfortable but I don't know why. A sort of cold feeling crawls all over me. I clutch my urn to my chest and hurry on.

I push the words out of my mind and think of something else. Phys. Ed. Tomorrow we will have to go to Phys. Ed. and all the boys will line up at the showers. I will get the Peter Hare, pubic hair treatment again. The boys will laugh and mock. I can't stand it. I just can't stand it. I am blushing just at the thought of it.

Maybe I can save myself with my mantra. Maybe the magic words will save me.

I still have some of the dust on my hands. I wipe it off and look around for something to concentrate on. There is a brick on the footpath. I will move it by strength of mind. 'Riah Devahs,' I say to myself. 'Riah Devahs.' I concentrate and concentrate on moving the brick while chanting my mantra to myself. Nothing happens. I try harder. 'Riah Devahs. Riah Devahs.'

It happens. It really happens. The brick starts to slide slowly along the path. It moves along as if pulled by an invisible magnet. This is incredible. Fantastic. I can make things move by thinking about it. As long as I am closing my eyes and saying my mantra.

I wonder if the magic words can help me with my pubic hair. I mean, if I concentrate and chant my mantra I might be able to get rid of it.

I close my eyes and start to concentrate on losing my pubic hair. 'Riah Devahs. Riah Devahs,' I say. After a bit I open my eyes and take a look down my jeans. But then I stop. I can feel someone looking at me. Someone is looking at me looking at my pubic hair.

It is Simons. And his mates. Now I am in for it. 'Still

122

there?' says Simons. The others all hoot with laughter.

'Please,' I say. 'I have to get home. Mum is ...'

'Mummy's boy,' says Simons. 'Mummy's hairy little boy.' He looks at the urn. He looks at it with a great deal of interest. 'What has little Pubic Hare got there?'

He starts to walk towards me. He is big and tough and I am skinny and weak. He is going to take my urn. I can't let that happen. I just can't. I grip the urn firmly in my hands. Then I close my eyes.

The gang start to laugh. 'No need to close your eyes, darling,' hoots Simons. 'We won't harm a hair on your ...'

I don't listen. I concentrate as hard as I can. I will get rid of them. I will say my mantra and get rid of them. I close my eyes. 'Riah Devahs,' I say to myself. 'Riah Devahs. They will steal my urn. They will take it away. I just know they will.' Rats, I am letting other thoughts into my mind. I must concentrate harder. 'Riah Devahs.' I say the words and think about getting rid of Simons and his gang. It is a real strain on my brain but I keep going with it.

There is a long silence. Then there is a shuffling noise. I still have the urn in my hands. I open my eyes. 'Hey,' says Simons. 'Hey, what's going on?' He rolls over on the ground waving his legs and arms up in the air. He looks just like a dog begging to be scratched on its tummy. The others do it too. They look ridiculous lying there on their backs on the ground. Their eyes are bulging out of their heads. They don't know what is going on. They don't know that it is me making them do it. I head off around the corner. Their angry voices fade off behind me. They will go back to normal once I am out of range.

I can't believe it. It works. It really works. I have made them lie on their backs and beg. Mind over matter. When I say the mantra and concentrate I can make things happen. I run for home as fast as I can.

Life is good. Well, at the moment it is anyway.

5

When I arrive home I cop it for being late for tea. But I don't care. I just smile and think about my new powers. I also think about Phys. Ed. in the morning and how I will be embarrassed in front of all the boys again.

After tea I go up to my bedroom and think about my problem. I check out my pubic hair.

What if I was to say my mantra and concentrate really hard? I might be able to make my pubic hair vanish by wishing it away. It is a good idea but it is filled with danger. What if something goes wrong? What if I made something else down there disappear by mistake? That would be terrible.

Or the wrong hair could vanish. Then I would be bald. No hair on top and too much down below. No, it is too risky. Much as I like the holy men I don't want to look like them. I will have to think of some other way of getting rid of the pubic hair. I am still not skilled enough with my mantra to risk changing my appearance.

There must be some other way of getting rid of the rotten hair.

An idea comes into my mind. Shaving. Dad shaves his face every day. I could shave my pubic hair off. Why didn't I think of it before? Simple.

I sneak off to Dad and Mum's bedroom and borrow Dad's electric razor. That will do the trick. I plug in the razor and it starts to buzz away like a hive of bees. I drop my pants and start to shave.

'Ow, ouch, ooh, ooh, ooh.' The pain is terrible. The long black hairs are caught in the razor. It is pulling and nipping at me. My eyes water. I scream out like crazy and dive for the switch. Click, it is off. The pain stops. Wonderful. But I still have a problem. The electric razor is stuck to me. Hairs are all fuzzled up into it. The electric razor clings on like a dog biting a shoe.

Just then Dad bursts into the room. His eyes grow wide when he sees the electric razor stuck to my private parts. 'Peter,' he yells. 'What on earth are you doing, boy?'

'Er, shaving,' I say.

'Shaving. You don't shave down there, lad.'

He comes into the room to remove the razor. He pulls and twists. 'Ouch,' I scream. Suddenly it comes away with bits of hair still sticking out. My eyes start to water with the pain. It hurts like crazy but I decide not to say anything. Not under the circumstances.

Finally, Dad sits down on the side of my bed. He gives me a talk. A long, long talk. About the birds and the bees and all that. It is all stuff I have heard before. But I nod and try to look interested. My mind is just not on it. I am thinking about Phys. Ed. and the showers. And how everyone will laugh at my pubic hair.

Finally Dad finishes his lecture and gets up to go. But his eye falls upon something. The urn. He picks it up and looks inside. 'What's this?' he says.

'Dust,' I say.

Dad stares for a long time. His mind is ticking over. 'This is not dust,' he says.

'No?' I say. 'What is it then?'

He utters the dreadful word. 'Ashes,' says Dad.

This word rings a bell in my mind. It takes a few seconds but finally I remember. The funeral. 'Ashes to ashes. Dust to dust.'

'Aargh,' I scream. 'It is human ashes. It is the final remains of . . . ' I look at the urn in horror. 'Riah Devahs.'

Tears rush down my face. My friend is gone for ever. He has moved on to a better place. All I have left of him is his ashes. And my mantra.

I tell Dad the whole story. Well, not the whole story. I don't tell him about concentrating. About how I can change things by willpower. I leave that bit out. But I tell him all the rest about how the holy men gave me the urn.

Dad nods and listens to my tale. He puts an arm around my shoulder. 'I am sorry you have lost your friend,' he says. 'But they should have known better. Giving human ashes to a boy. That's not right. We have to return these ashes to nature,' he says. 'You can't keep someone's remains in your bedroom.'

I think for a bit. What Dad says is true. Riah Devahs left me his urn and ashes as a puzzle. I had to find my own way. Work out the mantra. But now I have it I can return his ashes to nature like Dad says. 'What about the urn?' I ask. 'Can I keep that?'

Dad thinks for a bit. 'Okay,' he says. 'I guess that will be okay.'

Dad drives us out into a lonely part of the forest. We stop at a high cliff overlooking black gum trees far below. Stars twinkle in the sky. A faint breeze is blowing. Dad tips the urn upside down and the ashes scatter in the breeze.

'Look,' says Dad. 'The breeze is carrying the ashes into the outstretched limbs of the trees below. The forest is welcoming the holy man back to the earth from which he came.'

I didn't know Dad was a poet. It is all rather beautiful actually. I know that Riah Devahs would be pleased at what we have done.

'Ashes to ashes. Dust to dust,' I say.

Dad hands me a tissue. 'Wipe out the inside of the urn,' he says. 'I don't want any human ashes coming back to the house.'

I take the tissue and do what he says. Then I throw it away.

Dad frowns. 'Don't litter the forest,' he says. 'Put it in the bin at home.'

He is right. Riah Devahs would not like tissues floating around the bush. I pick it up and we head for home.

7

That night I have a peaceful sleep. Normally I would stay awake worrying about the Phys. Ed. class in the morning.

But I have my mantra to help me. I will use my magic words to save myself from embarrassment. Riah Devahs is gone for ever but his words are fixed firmly in my mind.

How will I use my magic words? What will I do? I think again about making my pubic hair vanish. Nah, it's still too risky. But there are plenty of other things I can do. I can use my powers to jam the lock on the shower room door. Then none of the boys or the Phys. Ed. teacher will be able to get in. Or I could turn the water to the showers off. Or maybe freeze the water in the pipes. Or, better still, I could make the Phys. Ed. teacher take a long walk in the bush. No, there is nothing to worry about any more. I sleep the sleep of a boy who knows what it is to be happy.

The next day we have Phys. Ed. We throw the shotput. We run laps of the oval. We kick the football. The usual stuff. Then, after it is all over, we head off for the showers. We file inside.

'Okay, boys,' says the Phys. Ed. teacher. 'Strip off and line up for the showers.'

I shut my eyes and start to concentrate. What will I do?

At the last minute I decide to get rid of my pubic hair after all. I don't want to be different. I want to be like everyone else. No, it is the best answer to my problem. I think about losing my pubic hair and start to chant my mantra. 'Riah Devahs. Riah Devahs.' I say to myself, all the time thinking about making my pubic hair vanish. I am nervous but I concentrate really hard. 'Riah Devahs.' I open my eyes and look down inside my shorts. Oh no. The hair is still there. It didn't work. Why didn't it work? Something is wrong.

128

The mind over matter didn't work. I still have a healthy stand of pubic hair. What is different? Why won't the words work now? Maybe it wasn't the words giving me the power. But what else could it be?

I decide to try it on something easy. I pull a hair out of my head. I take it out and put it on the bench. I concentrate on moving it. 'Riah Devahs. Riah Devahs,' I think to myself. My brain is nearly boiling with the effort but nothing happens. I have lost my power.

Now nothing can save me. I am about to be called Pubic Hare all over again. My private parts will be a public joke. I am history.

The other boys all start to undress. They don't seem to care about being in the nuddy. They just drop their pants and hang them up without a thought. Some of them have started to head towards the showers already. They don't have a pubic hair between them.

I can feel a sneeze coming on. I pull a tissue out of my pocket. A used tissue. I notice that it still has a few flakes of ashes clinging to it. It is the same tissue I used to clean out the urn. I tap the ashes onto my palm. It is all that is left of Riah Devahs. Ashes to ashes. Dust to dust.

I remember the first time I had ashes on my hand. And the time after that. Suddenly it hits me. Like a bolt of lightning. It wasn't the mantra giving me the power. It was the ashes. The power was coming from the last remains of Riah Devahs. Every time I concentrated I had ashes on my hand. And I still do. Only a few but it might work. You never know. It is worth a try. It is worth giving Riah one last try.

I think about my pubic hair. And how I am different

from everyone else. I get an idea. I will risk it. I close my eyes and concentrate. Boy, do I concentrate. I have never thought about anything so much in all my life. Talk about mind over matter. All I think about is pubic hair.

A sneeze is coming. I try to stop it. The last thing I need is a sneeze, especially when I have ashes on my palm. 'Ah, ah, tishoo.'

Did it work? I open my eyes and look. The ashes have gone. Sneezed away into oblivion. I will never be able to work my magic again. But it doesn't matter. Not if it worked. Not if my one last effort was successful.

I make a quick check inside my pants. It is still there. But I am not worried. Not one bit. Because it worked. Yes it worked. I am the same as everyone else. Yes, yes, yes.

No, that's not right. I am not the same as everyone else. They are all the same as me. Simons and all the other boys start to scream and cover up. They yell and shout and wrap towels around themselves. Each of them has a thick forest of pubic hair. It is long and curly and wonderful. They are shocked out of their brains. Their faces are so red you could warm your hands on them. None of the boys know where in the heck all the hair has come from.

But I do.

A Little Bit
From the Author
Part 7

I have only stolen something once in my life. I was six years old and I took a packet of hair pins from the lounge-room of the lady next door. They would have been worth about twenty cents, I guess.

That type of hair pin was only used by girls and women so I gave them to my mother. I also told a lie. I said, 'Look what I found on the footpath, Mum.'

Well, she was so pleased. 'Oh, you are a good boy,' she said. 'That's just what I need.' She went on and on and on about how clever and kind I was. The more she said the worse I felt. My conscience really gave me a bad time. The thought that I had done something wrong just wouldn't go away and it made me unhappy for ages. I was a thief. I felt so bad that I have never forgotten the incident.

When I was a teacher some of my students were talked into stealing a hosepipe by some big boys. They didn't know what to do with the hosepipe and in the end they threw it in a pond. Someone saw them and came and reported it to the school. They had to buy a new hosepipe and say sorry to the owner.

Both of these things happened a long time ago. But

last year I got to thinking about a guilty conscience. And how some people talk other people into stealing. It seemed like good material for a book.

So I wrote a book called *The Gizmo* about a boy who steals a gadget from the market. He throws it away but it follows him around. Like a guilty conscience.

These little events are the stuff of stories. I am always on the lookout for them.

Paul Jennings

About Paul Jennings

'The biggest sin in writing is to be boring.'
                                    Paul Jennings

Paul Jennings' amazing success story began in December 1985 when *Unreal!* was published. Within months it was on the bestseller lists and in every child's schoolbag, and there it has stayed. It's been the same with every book that followed.

Spooky, funny, naughty, yucky, always wacky and always with a surprise ending, Paul's stories are devoured by readers of all ages. Every year his books top the lists of nominations for the Australian state awards chosen by children. In 1992, Paul won an award in every children's choice list throughout Australia and in 1993, the top eight books in the KROC Awards were all Paul Jennings titles.

In 1990, a thirteen-part television series based on Paul's early stories was screened in Australia and in the UK. *Round the Twist*, the series and the book, received critical acclaim from both countries. In 1993, the second series of *Round the Twist* was screened in Australia and the UK, where it was the top-rating children's program. Both series have since been screened in over forty countries throughout the world. Paul wrote the screenplays for both series and each time he won an AWGIE (Australian

Writers' Guild) Award for the best Children's Adaptation (TV). The second series was also a finalist in the 1993 International EMMY Awards. The episode 'Little Squirt' won the Best Children's TV Drama in the 1993 Australian Film Institute Awards.

Other awards and commendations include: *Uncanny!* (shortlisted for the 1989 NSW Premier's Literary Award for Children's Books); *Unmentionable!* (shortlisted for the 1992 NSW State Literary Awards); and *Grandad's Gifts*, illustrated by Peter Gouldthorpe (shortlisted for the 1993 Children's Book Council of Australia Picture Book of the Year Award). In the ABPA (Australian Book Publishers' Association) Awards in 1993, *Spooner or Later*, Paul's hilarious and inventive collaboration with Ted Greenwood and Terry Denton, won two awards: the Joyce Nicholson Award for the Best Designed Book and the Award for the Best Designed Children's Book of the Year. Their next collaboration, *Duck for Cover*, was shortlisted for the 1995 CBC Book of the Year Awards. In 1993, Paul was nominated for Victorian of the Year and in the 1995 Australia Day Honours List he was made a Member of the Order of Australia for services to children's literature.

Paul Jennings has written over eighty stories and has sold more than two million copies of his books. He receives thousands of fan letters every year and replies to them all (if they include a return address).

'Jennings has found the perfect formula for the scary and supernatural sprinkled with just the right touch of hilarity . . . Don't miss out on the fun here.'
    School Library Journal (USA), starred review for *Unreal!*